Orange Public Library
Orange, NJ

Gift

Do you want to buy a
(or almost any) book?
"Special Order" it for
Most current books are available

D1156712

Deadline:
2 A.M.

By Robert L. Pike

DEADLINE: 2 A.M.
BANK JOB
THE GREMLIN'S GRAMPA
REARDON
POLICE BLOTTER

THE QUARRY
MUTE WITNESS
  (MYSTERY WRITERS OF AMER-
  ICA EDGAR AWARD WINNER)

José Da Silva Novels by Robert L. Fish

TROUBLE IN PARADISE
THE GREEN HELL TREASURE
THE XAVIER AFFAIR
THE BRIDGE THAT WENT NOWHERE
ALWAYS KILL A STRANGER
BRAZILIAN SLEIGH RIDE

THE DIAMOND BUBBLE
THE SHRUNKEN HEAD
ISLE OF THE SNAKES
THE FUGITIVE
  (M.W.A. EDGAR AWARD WIN-
  NER)

By the Same Author

EVERY CRIME IN THE BOOK
  (M.W.A. ANTHOLOGY)
THE MEMOIRS OF
  SCHLOCK HOMES
THE WAGER
RUB-A-DUB-DUB
TRICKS OF THE TRADE
WHIRLIGIG
WITH MALICE TOWARDS ALL
  (M.W.A. ANTHOLOGY)
THE MURDER LEAGUE
THE HOCHMANN MINIATURES

THE INCREDIBLE SCHLOCK HOMES
THE TRIALS OF O'BRIEN
THE ASSASSINATION BUREAU
  (COMPLETION OF AN UNFIN-
  ISHED WORK BY JACK LON-
  DON)
THE HANDY DEATH
  (IN COLLABORATION WITH
  HENRY ROTHBLATT)
WEEKEND '33
  (IN COLLABORATION WITH
  BOB THOMAS)

PROPERTY OF THE
ORANGE N.J. PUBLIC LIBRARY
IE LIBRARY NEEDS & WELCOMES GIFTS & BEQUESTS

Deadline: 2 A.M.

A Lieutenant Reardon Novel

by ROBERT L. PIKE

DOUBLEDAY & COMPANY, INC.
GARDEN CITY, NEW YORK   1976

FREE PUBLIC LIBRARY
NUTLEY, NEW JERSEY

All of the characters in this book are fictitious and any resemblance to actual persons, living or dead, is purely coincidental.

ISBN: 0-385-03563-2
Library of Congress Catalog Card Number 75-17073
Copyright © 1976 by Robert L. Fish
ALL RIGHTS RESERVED
PRINTED IN THE UNITED STATES OF AMERICA
FIRST EDITION

7
Copy 1

This book is affectionately dedicated
with friendship and respect
to
Gerard–"Jerry"–Rothbart
World traveler, fascinating conversationalist,
indefatigable pub crawler; a man who in today's
world actually reads books and enjoys them; and
God's gift to the telephone companies of the
world.
Who could say more?

Deadline:
2 A.M.

CHAPTER 1

PROPERTY OF THE
ORANGE N.J. PUBLIC LIBRARY
THE LIBRARY NEEDS & WELCOMES GIFTS & BEQUESTS

Friday—8:45 P.M.

Sergeant Michael Holland sat extremely still and tried to make out as much of the man's features in the rear-view mirror as he could. Night had fallen within the hour and the only illumination came from the reflected light of a streetlamp a few yards down the block, plus the occasional glow from the cigar tucked in one corner of the man's bearded mouth.

Sergeant Holland's first thought at being accosted in his own car in his own driveway had been that some of the boys from the Hall of Justice were playing a practical joke on him on this, the day of his retirement from the force; but another look into the mirror revealed a strange, casually cruel, faintly smiling bearded face, cigar atilt, that instantly disabused him of the notion. Holland had no idea of how the man had managed to get into the rear seat of the locked car, nor when; but he recognized the authority of the cold muzzle against his neck and accordingly kept his hands pressed tightly on his knees. In addition to the sardonic cast of the full lips gripping the cigar, the small mirrored glass showed enough of the weapon held in the gloved hand to be instantly recognized. Mike Holland knew the gun well. It was a .38 caliber police positive, and until five o'clock that afternoon, one just like it had been as much a part of him as his right arm.

1

Michael Holland had spent a portion of his career on the San Francisco police force teaching recruits how properly to use precisely this weapon. He knew the damage it could do to a two-inch plank in the ballistics lab, and in the course of the few years he had spent in Homicide before being shunted to Communications to work out his final years, he had also seen the damage it could do to the human body. That damage was considerable. It was not easy to forget.

He cleared his throat, surprised when he spoke that his voice was not even tighter than it was. "What goes on?"

"Relax," the man said amusedly. "Keep quiet and keep still." The voice was calm, detached. He took the cigar from his mouth, flicked ashes to the floor almost contemptuously, and replaced the cigar. The pistol never moved from Holland's neck.

"But—"

"I said, quiet."

Mike Holland sighed and glanced about, moving his head with extreme caution, feeling the muzzle scrape lightly against his neck, but being most careful in keeping his hands on his knees. From the house on the right, his own, he could see the faint glow of the lamp he always left lit whenever he went out evenings, for Michael Holland lived alone and had since his Katherine had died eight years before. And to the left the Horvath place was dark, as he expected, since Steve and Margaret were off someplace on vacation. Los Angeles, he remembered, and then thought how unimportant it was, any more than it was important that the other houses around held neighbors who were not on vacation. It would take quite a shout on his part to be heard over Walter Cronkite, or whoever—even assuming anyone would come if they heard him. Or if he'd even be alive when they got there. The man in the mirror, with that faint smile on his kisser, looked just wild enough, with all that hair, to use the revolver just to hear the bang.

Mike Holland wet his lips, and wondered what they were waiting for. He glanced into the mirror, read nothing in the steady eyes that stared back at him, and brought his attention to the closed garage ahead. Take it easy, he told himself. Don't let yourself get up-tight. This clown has to be making a mistake. And the guy in the mirror, despite that slightly off-beat smile, still didn't look like a hophead—although Mike Holland had to admit it was getting pretty hard to tell these days, what with the drug companies coming out with new pills every half hour, bless their little commercial hearts. He looked back up into the mirror.

"What's this all about? What are we waiting for? What do you want? Who are you?"

As if in answer to his questions, the door beside him suddenly opened and he saw that his assailant had not been alone. A second man appeared in the opening, thin to the point of emaciation, abnormally short, his face hidden in the shadows of an excessively wide hat brim. "Nobody around," the newcomer said in a deep gravelly voice that seemed odd coming from his stunted body. "Just what I like—a nice quiet neighborhood." He turned his head in Holland's direction. "Okay," he said. "Feet first."

Mike Holland stared, not understanding. "What about my feet?"

The thin man seemed to double over, and for a stunned moment Holland hoped it was with pain, but then he realized with sudden fury that while he had been staring at the weird-looking hat and hoping the little bastard had suffered a burst appendix, the skinny little son-of-a-bitch had clamped a set of cuffs about his ankles.

"Hey!" Mike Holland said, outraged, and started to reach. The gun instantly was thrust with force against his neck and Holland froze. This was no Saturday-night special, a four-buck job that maybe it went off and maybe it didn't. This one served for the police, and this one went off each and every time, without fail.

"Hands," the little man said evenly, and looked up at the large sergeant. In the reflected light from the streetlamp, Mike was able at last to make out the face. The eyes beneath that ridiculous hat brim were sunken, as were the nose and cheeks. The whole effect was like seeing two burned holes in a scarred and ravaged barrel stave, and somehow reminded Mike Holland of pictures he had seen one time of lepers. He looks like a very sick kid with his old man's hat on him, Mike thought with sudden anger; a fifty-year-old bastard kid who ought to have that stupid hat jammed over his stupid ears and then given a good healthy kick in the butt for luck.

"Hands," the little man repeated.

Mike fought down growing anger, knowing temper could only be a mistake.

"Now, look, you characters," he said in as reasonable a tone as he could muster. "I got a sum total of maybe thirty bucks on me, and the car's practically worthless. I don't even carry theft insurance on her. She's damn near as old as I am." Or anyway, as I feel, he thought bitterly. You didn't retire out of the force one day too soon, Holland, he thought, getting picked up like a farmer his first night in a topless joint! "And there's not a thin dime in the house, either," Mike went on, "plus my son's in there asleep, a Medal of Honor winner, and if you wake him up over some nonsense like this, he'll take that toy pistol away from you and push it in one of your ears and pull it out the other!" And he would have, too, if Michael Patrick Holland, Jr., hadn't died at the age of four from what they called the croup in those days. "Take the lousy thirty bucks and leave me be," Mike Holland said wearily. "I got an appointment tonight."

The little man had been listening to this story with the air of a person who had gone into a jewelry store to buy a cheap watch strap and found himself the unwilling participant in an auction. He snapped out of his reverie.

"Hands," he said evenly. "Out in front of you. And keep them together."

"Now listen, you dumb baboons!" Mike Holland said furiously, no longer able to contain his ire. "I'm a police officer and you guys are asking for more trouble than you can handle! Sweet Mary and Jesus! Take the lousy thirty bucks and pray to your saints I don't never run into either one of you two again. . . !"

There was the sudden wiping of the gunsight against the burly neck. The gunsight had either been given a poor tumbling job at the factory, or had been sharpened by its sadistic owner to serve as a weapon on its own. Holland felt the chilling pain, the sudden automatic cold tightening of the scrotum at the thought of flesh being parted by edged steel, and then the dampness of blood, warm blood, his blood, running down his collar. His first thought was that his nice new white shirt, bought especially for the occasion of the evening, would be ruined; but then he knew it really didn't matter. It didn't look as if he were going to get to any dinner tonight, anyway.

"Hands," the little man repeated for the third time in that oddly inconsistent rasping voice. His tone was not remonstrating, merely reminding. Mike Holland took a deep breath and brought his big hands forward slowly, fighting down the impulse to take the scrawny neck before him and wring it like a dishrag, but he had no doubt that the bearded bastard with the cigar behind him wouldn't hesitate to use the gun. Mike brought his hands together and felt the cold steel snap around his thick wrists.

"Over," the small man said in that same impersonal tone, and made a move to enter the car. Mike stared at the familiar dashboard as if seeing it for the first time, and then slowly edged his large body toward the other side of the car. He knew he should be making mental notes on the two hoods, burning details into his trained memory beyond the mere fact that one was skinny and had poor taste in hats, and the other was bearded, smoked cigars, and was nasty, but at the moment his anger blotted out the ability to act properly. Besides, his neck hurt, although not half as much as his pride. Taken like a child! The fact that he had climbed into his car quite naturally and suddenly found a gun put on him had nothing to do with the matter; somehow he should never have allowed himself to be suckered like that!

The skinny little man slid into the driver's seat, pushed down on the adjusting button and slid the seat closer to the steering wheel to accommodate his reduced size, reached up a skeletal hand to adjust the rear-view mirror to his satisfaction, reached out to do the same for the side-view mirror, and then squirmed into a more comfortable position. The skin-tight gloves he wore made him appear to have brown hands attached to pale thin wrists. The bearded man took his cigar from his mouth and leaned over, bringing his lips close to Mike Holland's ear.

"We can do this the easy way or the hard way," he said softly.

"I can lay this gun barrel alongside your ear and put you to sleep, and then we'll just be two pals taking a drunken friend home. And you'll wake up with the large, economy-sized hangover. Or we can go along just the way we are without any big disturbance from you, and you may even live to see the grandchildren from that Medal of Honor son you don't have." The gun snaked forward, pressing cruelly against the cut, and then was partially withdrawn. Mike winced involuntarily. The quiet voice went on. "It's that simple. Take your choice."

Mike remained silent. The bearded man seemed to take it as acceptance.

"Good," he said pleasantly, and tucked his cigar back in place. He looked toward the small driver. "Let's get going. We're behind schedule, listening to Sergeant Holland, here, tell us how he's a policeman."

"Yeah," the little man said with a grin. "I thought he was a streetcar conductor without his uniform, myself." He turned on the ignition, listening to the steady purring of the old motor in appreciation for the obvious attention it had received, and then put on the lights, put the car into gear, and backed from the driveway. "Not bad for an old clunker," he said to no one in particular, and swung the wheel. He changed gears and started down the street, driving with obvious skill, but with equally obvious care.

The man in the back seat spoke, a small edge to his voice. "A little faster, Harry, if you don't mind?"

"What's the difference we're a couple minutes late?" Harry asked, but nevertheless he pressed the accelerator a trifle. The car responded, moving a bit faster.

"We made a schedule, let's stick to it," the bearded man said, and lapsed into silence, sucking silently on his cigar.

In the front seat, Mike Holland tried to remember, in recent months—or even years, for that matter—whom he might have so enraged as to account for being picked up and treated in this manner. From his personal life? But he had never been a mixer, had never had trouble of any kind with his neighbors, and had spent nineteen out of twenty evenings watching television, with an occasional night out for the movies to break the monotony. And it certainly could be nothing connected with women. Before Katie's death Mike had felt no need even to look at another woman, and since her death, he had felt no desire to.

From his professional life? Well, in Communications one scarcely played any role in an important case serious enough to warrant revenge; and his days in Homicide were so far back that Mike doubted these two were more than kids in those days. Besides, even when he was in Homicide, as Mike Holland himself would have been the first to admit, he had never done anything startling; it was one of the reasons he was still a sergeant when he had been retired that afternoon after over forty years of service. The sad fact was that nobody whom the other men called "Pop" —some damn near as old as he was—had ever done anything he could recall that could possibly result in such demonstrated enmity. So what in the name of sweet Mary and Jesus could be the reason for picking him up?

The bearded man rolled down the window on his side of the car, tossed out his cigar, and rolled the window back in place. He leaned his wrist against the glass, trying to read the time by the light of a passing lamppost. He finally managed to see the watch hands and looked up at the driver with a frown.

"Let's get a little more speed out of this wagon, shall we, Harry?"

"Let's not get picked up for speeding," the little man said, and then added hastily, "That's what you told me, remember?"

The bearded man accepted this recognition of his leadership.

"I know what I told you," he said with a touch of impatience. "Now I'm suggesting we don't get stopped for loitering, or for obstructing traffic. Move it!"

"Right." The thin man speeded the car up again. He glanced over at their prisoner. "He's bleeding all over the car," he said conversationally.

"So let him bleed," the bearded man said indifferently. "It's his blood. And his car." He leaned back, the revolver dangling

7

indolently from one finger, his other hand stroking his full beard thoughtfully. His eyes were fixed on the blood welling from the cut on Mike Holland's neck, but his thoughts were already on step two of his daring scheme.

CHAPTER 2

Friday—9:20 P.M.

Lieutenant James Reardon, nursing a brand of cognac he normally would never have considered ordering, primarily for economic reasons, sat back in his chair at the head table and thought that if noise made an affair a success, then the party being thrown for the retirement of Sergeant Michael Patrick Holland had to be the achievement of the year. Some clown on the entertainment committee—as Reardon recalled, that had been the responsibility of Burglary—had managed to locate a jukebox, and the lieutenant only hoped they hadn't swiped it. In fact, he wished they hadn't found it at all; but they had, and they had dragged it into the sacrosanct precincts of the back room of Marty's Oyster House, and some other clown had fed the monster a fistful of quarters, and if the thing had a volume control, nobody had located it. Or, more likely, nobody had even bothered to look for it. At the moment, fortunately, the machine was delivering itself of a Hawaiian love song, so the racket was less deafening, although the difference in decibels was easily made up for by the loud guffawing of a group from Traffic who were over at the temporary bar probably telling Polish traffic jokes, if there were such things.

Lieutenant Reardon was in the Homicide Division of the San Francisco police, and as a general rule enjoyed his work very

9

much. He was a stocky athletic-looking man in his early thirties, with thick russet hair, a rugged yet remarkably sensitive face, and with sharp intelligent gray eyes. At the moment a deep groove between those eyes outlined a frown. Where the devil was Pop Holland? Reardon was not worried that the meal would be spoiled because the guest of honor was late; Marty's Oyster House, whose front dining room boasted the finest cuisine in all San Francisco, had a standard dinner for affairs held in the back room, apparently designed to discourage people from ever holding an affair there again. But what might well happen, the lieutenant knew, was not a question of whether the rubber chicken with plastic peas was up—or down—to standard; the problem was that any further tardiness was apt to result in the guests being too far gone with liquor to partake of the fare. Which, thinking about it, might not be such a tragedy at that.

There was movement at his side and he looked up to see his good friend and co-worker Sergeant Dondero pulling up a chair beside him. Dondero, two years younger than Reardon, was one inch shorter and thirty pounds heavier, an increase in weight he claimed came about when he stopped smoking in a bet with Stan Lundahl, also of the department. It was a bet Dondero had won, to his intense sorrow. Reardon smiled, pleased to see the other.

"I thought you were still on vacation, Don. When did you get back?"

"This afternoon. Think I'd miss Pop's retirement party? With free booze?" Dondero smiled at Reardon affectionately. "How's the old married man?"

Reardon's smile faded. "We didn't get married."

Dondero's smile changed to a puzzled frown. "What do you mean, you didn't get married?"

"What does it sound like? We didn't get married, that's all."

"But you phoned me from Tahoe! You said you were up there with Jan, you were going to get married—"

"I know what I said. But Jan changed her mind."

"Changed her mind? Why?" Dondero sounded more put out about it than his friend.

"Skip it," Reardon said wearily. "It's a long story and one I'd rather not go into right now."

"But—"

Reardon's eyes hardened. "Let's drop it?"

"But—oh, sure, if you insist," Dondero said, and then brightened. "Hey, maybe if I talk to Jan? You know she always pays more attention to me than she does to you—" He saw the look on Reardon's face and grinned. "I was just joking, pal."

"Very funny!"

"We can't hit zingers all the time," Dondero said, and looked around the room. "Where's Pop?"

"I haven't a clue."

"The story of your life," Dondero said sadly, "and a pretty sad confession for a so-called detective." He studied the room again, and frowned. "It's not like Pop to be late, especially for his own party." He looked about the room for a third time and was struck by a sudden thought. "Hey! If all the cops in town are here, who's minding the store?"

"They aren't all here," Reardon said sourly. "Pop isn't."

"Well, outside of him—"

Reardon shrugged, his good humor returning. "Maybe all the crooks are having an affair of their own over on the other side of town."

"Well," Dondero said expressively, "if they are, I hope for their sake the service is better than it is here. How do you get a drink in this dump? And who in their right mind ever picked this place for the dinner, anyway?" He came to his feet, shaking his head. "A guy could die of thirst. Hold the fort while I raid the bar. Another for you?"

"Remy Martin."

"In a water glass," Dondero said, and moved away.

Reardon looked after him. He felt like he'd like to take it in a water glass. After all, the very least the chairman of the dinner committee ought to be able to do was to get his fair share of the liquor allocation, or anyway before Traffic drank it all up. He studied the crowded room with a faint air of proprietorship, although now that Dondero had reminded him, he wondered why indeed he had selected Marty's Oyster House for the festivities. If he thought the waiters at Marty's would change their habits merely because a cop was being honored, he should have known better. Possibly if a cop was being dishonored? Probably not even then. The waiters at Marty's operated on the principle that, right or wrong, the customer was always neglectable.

As if to refute that uncharitable thought, a waiter pushed through to his side. For a moment Reardon wondered if he should apologize to the aproned figure, but he was saved the necessity because the waiter was busy making a circular motion with one hand, as if he were cranking some imaginary object, while his other hand, curled, was pressed tightly against his ear. It was the time-honored charade to indicate someone was wanted on the telephone, and even as Reardon came to his feet he wondered how the ancient pantomime had ever managed to survive. What it actually looked like, he thought, was that the waiter wanted him to come to the kitchen and listen to the meat grinder.

A sudden thought came and he moved with greater alacrity, a broad smile beginning to change his face. Jan, of course! Calling to apologize, probably, although he was magnanimous enough to realize no apology was necessary. He started to follow the waiter and almost ran down Dondero, carefully balancing a drink in each hand. Dondero paused to proffer one, but Reardon shook his head.

"Later," he said, raising his voice over the din. "There's a phone call for me."

Dondero noted the fatuous grin. "Jan?"

"Probably. I hope," Reardon said, and raised crossed fingers.

"Then I'll tag along. You'll need moral support. And with me there you won't say anything you'll be sorry for afterward."

"And you're also nosey."

"That, too," Dondero said agreeably, and followed along, balancing the drinks carefully.

The waiter paused at the entrance to a corridor leading from the hall, to make sure his trail-blazing had not been in vain, saw Reardon and Dondero close behind, and led the way to a small unmarked door at the end of the narrow hallway. The waiter opened the door, closed it after their entrance, and then hurried back to take his place once again near the thick of the crowd.

12

After all, one could hardly ignore customers unless one were near at hand, could one? Obviously not.

Inside the office Reardon was pleasantly surprised to find that Marty, no fool, had soundproofed the room and that the bedlam of the back room had disappeared as soon as the door had been closed. "That's better," he said with grateful relief, and raised the receiver from the desk blotter, making no attempt to hide the eagerness in his voice. "Jan?"

A strange masculine voice was on the line. "Lieutenant Reardon?"

Reardon swallowed his disappointment. "Speaking." Another possible explanation for the call suddenly occurred to him, an explanation equally disturbing. "Is this in regard to Pop Holland? Is something wrong with him?"

"I don't know about wrong," the voice said apologetically, "but I'm afraid Sergeant Holland won't be able to make your party tonight. I'm extending his regrets for him." There was a strange touch of amusement in the even, semicultured voice.

"What? Who is this?"

"Just call me a friend—"

"Well, listen, friend," Reardon said, in no mood for mysteries at the moment. "Put Mike Holland on the line, will you?"

"I'm afraid that's not allowed," the voice said with false regret. "You see, he's been kidnapped."

Reardon shook his head in annoyance. These gagsters could be a pain in the butt at times.

"Look, friend," he said with a patience he was far from feeling, "just put Mike on the phone, will you?"

"You're not paying attention," the other man said reprovingly. "You're not keeping your ears open. I said, Mike Holland is being held captive, and therefore is unable to appear at your little wing-ding—"

Reardon took a deep breath. He had about had it.

"Now look, chum," he said firmly. "Fun's fun, but this isn't any college fraternity initiation we're holding here. I've got forty-eight characters getting stewed to the ears, waiting for Pop to show up.

13

And we all have lots of vital things to do tomorrow—like golf, for instance, or even go to work for the less fortunate—and we'd all like to get home in reasonable time to sober up. So will you please tell Mike Holland to quit fooling around and get his butt over here? Right now?"

"You still refuse to understand," the voice said, and there was the slightest touch of disappointment in the tone, as if in sincere regret for Reardon's thick-headedness. "I am quite serious. I said that Sergeant Michael Holland has been kidnapped. By us. I mean it. He has been abducted. Spirited off. Snatched, if you prefer the vernacular."

Reardon opened his mouth to say something, and then closed it again. He looked at the phone in a slightly dazed manner and tried again.

"Just what in hell are you talking about?"

"What an oddly neutral response!" the man said, and sounded quite sincere. He sighed. "Still, I suppose it's understandable. You're probably half in the bag yourself, by this time. I knew we shouldn't have delayed this call, but poor old Sergeant Holland insisted on telling us the story of his life. As he saw it, of course."

Reardon gritted his teeth. "Look, pal! What sort of a gag is this?"

"My, you *are* stubborn, aren't you? Here—possibly this will help to convince you." There was a slight pause; then in a muffled but clearly recognizable tone, Reardon heard, ". . . *listen, you dumb baboons! I told you before, I'm a police officer! I don't know who you think you got, but I'm a cop! Can't you get it through your thick skulls? Now who in the name of sweet Mary and Jesus is going to give a plugged dime for an old cop . . . ?*" The voice returned. "Recognize it? I'm sure you do. Taped just moments ago." The voice turned sardonically apologetic. "The fidelity isn't all one might wish, but it's a new recorder and I expect it will take a little time to get used to it."

Reardon realized that Dondero was standing beside him, drinks in hand, staring at him with an odd expression on his face. He cupped the mouthpiece without removing the receiver from his ear.

14

"Get on another phone and trace this call!"

Dondero didn't waste precious time asking questions, he put the drinks on the desk hastily, slopping good liquor on the blotter, and hurried from the room, dragging the thick door closed behind him. Reardon returned to his call, trying to sound the same.

"I'm not sure I got everything you were trying to say, chum. You were saying about Pop Holland . . . ?"

There was a delicious laugh from the telephone.

"Lieutenant, you are delightful! Not subtle, not particularly bright, but delightful! Your delay in answering was obvious, not to mention the fact that the tone changes slightly when one puts his hand over the mouthpiece and speaks. So I can only assume you were relaying the situation to a confederate, and asking him to trace the call, no doubt." The laugh was repeated, delicate, refined, sardonic. "You know, you're not as familiar with Marty's Oyster House as you should be. They have only the one telephone, and you're using it. The one on the maître d's desk is an extension, you know. And the nearest other telephone is a block away, and I'm afraid when your friend gets to it, he'll find it out of order. A pity, but we had to do it. On the other hand, we own no shares in A.T.&T. And, of course, I'll be long gone from this booth before your friend can locate any other means of tracing me."

Reardon stared at the instrument, feeling helpless. There wasn't even a squad car around for its radio; it had been decided it would look better for the public if the patrol cars were left where they belonged, either in service or in the garage, and not around Marty's, looking like a raid.

"What do you want?"

"Oh, that?" The man sounded surprised that it had taken Reardon so long to come to the point. "Well, we didn't want all you dedicated public servants to waste an entire evening waiting for Sergeant Holland, when he won't be able to attend. Much better you should all be out on the streets protecting us citizens from those nasty criminals, you know . . ."

"You bastard!"

"Language," said the other man, and laughed genially.

15

Reardon brought his temper under control. One day, he promised himself, he'd get his hands on this joker, and that would be time enough either for language or reprisals.

"All right," he said tightly. "What do you want?"

"I just told you—"

"For Pop Holland!"

"Oh, that! Well, you'll receive a tape in the morning mail, Lieutenant, addressed to you. It seems to be the modern method of relaying demands. The tape will explain our requirements quite clearly. And now, I'm afraid I can't stay on the line much longer. Your friend might know of a telephone in the neighborhood that I don't."

"Hold on a second—"

"And one more thing . . ." The voice turned cold, deadly serious. "Let's keep the newspapers out of this. Or any other medium. That's if you care for Holland's health."

"Don't hang up—"

"I'm afraid I must. So good-bye. Or, better, *au revoir*." There was the briefest of pauses, then a faint laugh, the caller's good humor restored. "And, of course, considering your banquet—*bon appetit*."

There was a quiet *click* as the other man placed the receiver in its cradle gently. Reardon pumped the button furiously, and then forced himself to refrain from attacking the instrument long enough to permit the telephone to respond with a dial tone. He dialed for the operator quickly, and waited. And waited and waited and waited. At long last the distant ringing stopped and a bored voice came on the line.

"This is your operator. May I help you?"

Reardon managed to bite back his first furious comment.

"Yes! This is the Police Department. We want to have a call traced."

"One moment. I'll connect you with the supervisor . . ."

"*Wait* . . . !" Too late! God, Reardon thought savagely, glaring at the instrument, where do they dredge up some of these zombies, anyway? There was another prolonged bout of ringing somewhere in limbo, while Reardon fumed helplessly. Then, when he was on the verge of ripping the instrument from the wall and stomping on it, the receiver at the other end was finally lifted.

"Supervisor . . ."

Reardon took a deep breath, trying to moderate his tone of voice.

"Supervisor, *this is urgent!* My name is Lieutenant Reardon of the Police Department. We want a call traced. It was made"—he consulted his watch—"at 10:02. Terminated, that is. The call was made to the number 664-0398. The party disconnected a few minutes ago." Or maybe more, he thought bitterly, considering the time it takes any of you clowns down at the phone company to lift a receiver!

"Was it a toll call or a local call?"

Good God! "I haven't the slightest idea. There weren't any coins dropped, if that's what you mean." The situation came back to him. "And you're wasting time, damn it!"

"If it was a toll call," the woman said, not at all perturbed by the thought of wasting time, nor at all prodded by the note of urgency in the other's voice, "then we can check it. Unless, of course, it was made from a public booth, in which case I'm afraid it would be very difficult—"

"Look, miss, damn it! Will you . . . ?"

"But you said you heard no coins drop, didn't you? Well, we'll do what we can. What number did you say the call was made to?"

Reardon gritted his teeth. "664-0398! Look, miss—"

"And that's in the city proper?"

"Yes, damn it! It's in the city! It's a restaurant, Marty's Oyster House! Look—"

"And to whom am I speaking?"

Reardon started to close his eyes and count to ten, or possibly a hundred, but then he realized he would only be aiding and abetting the imbecile in wasting time.

"My name is Reardon," he said, amazed at his calmness and wondering how long it could last, "Lieutenant James Reardon. Of the Homicide Division," he added significantly, hoping this fact might startle the woman into some form of useful activity. "And now, would you please get started on—"

"And what number are you calling from?"

"Goddamn it! I told you a dozen times! 664-0398!"

"You didn't say that was the number you were using. You said that was the number where the call was received," the woman said primly, overlooking his language since she was a lady. Reardon bit his lip. So he hadn't told her exactly, but if she had enough brains to come out from under a falling safe, she could have figured it out. "In any event," the woman went on calmly, "I'm afraid we can only trace calls when the authority to have the trace placed comes through the Police Department. Directly, that is," she added, forestalling any argument, "from the Communications Center at the Hall of Justice."

"What do you mean, directly? I'm a police officer! My shield number—"

"I mean, we have no means of identifying you as a police officer over the telephone, I'm afraid."

"Miss," Reardon said with a patience he was far from feeling, "who else would want a call traced, except the police?"

"Many people," the supervisor said, and sniffed loudly at the memory of irate husbands and cheating wives, not to mention cheating husbands and irate wives. It was one of the major reasons she had never married, and nobody was ever going to convince her there were any other reasons. "I'm sorry, but if you'll relay your request through proper police channels, we'll be glad to see what we can do—"

Her tone clearly indicated that in her opinion if he was a policeman, she was Greta Garbo. Reardon stared at the wall. Well, the chances of tracing the call after this delay were undoubtedly zero in any event.

"Miss," he said wearily. "What's your name?"

"I'm afraid we're not permitted to give out that information."

"Now, look!" he began furiously, and then gave up. "Forget it," he said, and dropped the receiver with a bang just as Dondero came back into the room in a rush, panting.

"Damn nearest phone's a block away and the damn thing doesn't work. Was going to cut in on you from the cashier's desk, but I figured it would just screw things up. Just once I'd like to

18

see a street phone that hasn't been ripped off! Or a patrol car when you need one! Anyway, I figured you'd be off the line by this time . . ."

Reardon was still trying to bring himself under control. The day he bought stock in A.T.&T. would be a cold one in Panama, although it would be wonderful to be on the board of directors just long enough to fire about two million operators and supervisors.

"Never mind," he said, and picked up the receiver again. "It's probably about a week too late now, in any case." He clicked the button several times. "And *now* where in hell's the dial tone?"

"What gives?" Dondero asked, and picked up his waiting drink, marveling that it was still there after his absence. And not only his, but Reardon's as well. Amazing! "What was all that mishagas about tracing the call? And all that about Pop?"

Reardon suddenly realized he also had a drink waiting. He picked it up, drank it down in one healthy gulp, shuddered a bit, and set the glass down. He also suddenly realized that Dondero didn't know what the whole thing was all about.

"Pop Holland's been kidnapped," he said somberly, holding the receiver to his ear, wondering if he might have broken the idiot apparatus when he had smashed the receiver down. "Snatched." Where the hell *was* the bloody dial tone?

"What?"

"That's what the man said. He wasn't fooling. He had Pop on tape." The dial tone was suddenly in his ear and for a moment Reardon wondered if it had been there all along. Wake up, he advised himself sternly, and dialed a number.

Dondero was staring at him unbelievingly.

"Who the devil would want to kidnap Pop? Why, for Christ's sake? He doesn't have an enemy in the world—"

"I doubt it was a friend."

Dondero hadn't even heard. ". . . and as far as dough is concerned, he's got no family, and outside his pension and the house, I doubt he's got five bills in the bank! So, why . . . ?"

A sexy, feminine voice answered the telephone. Reardon stared, and then barked into the telephone:

"Who's this?"

19

There was a giggle. "It's your nickel. You tell me first," the sexy voice said, wheedlingly. "Who are you?"

"Damn!" Reardon said, and hung up, warning himself not to allow the phone company to get him down. Your nickel! He had to get octogenarian sex pots on his wrong numbers, yet! He clicked for the dial tone for what seemed to be the hundredth time, feeling as if he had spent the last three years of his life on the phone.

Dondero looked at him. "Who you calling?"

"The Hall, of course. Like I should have right off the bat." He stared at Dondero sourly. "And don't ask me if the kidnapper didn't tell me not to contact the police . . ."

"Who, me?" Dondero was shocked. "Joke at a time like this?"

"You," Reardon said. The dial tone came on and he finally managed to dial the proper number. "Go out and tell the guys the news. Let them eat and go home, or just go home. And then come back." It was going to be a long, long night, he knew, and it would undoubtedly be made a lot longer by the fact that a large part of it would probably be spent in using the blaggedy blanged blumpery blithery instrument in his hand.

CHAPTER 3

Saturday—1:10 A.M.

Frank Paul Oliver—Porky Frank or Porky Oliver to his friends, depending upon the closeness of the relationship—was a businessman with various interests, and one of his interests, in a minor fashion, was the collecting of information. It was not his principal business; his major interest was in running a small but honest handbook, but when in the course of his daily endeavors he ran into facts that could have a monetary value, Porky quite properly collected those facts and eventually sold them. To have done otherwise would have been unbusinesslike, and contrary to the "Waste Not, Want Not" philosophy instilled in him as a youth by an equally businesslike mother.

The standard word for a person who indulges in the sale of information for money is "stool pigeon," but the word carries the wrong connotation. Years of conditioning by television, the movies, and cheap novels have left the public with the mental picture of a stool pigeon as a small, cringing man, usually with a terminal cough, dressed in a crumpled suit with frayed cuffs and upturned jacket collar, who whispers hoarsely from the corner of his mouth, normally past a stained cigarette plastered to his lower lip. Frank Paul Oliver would have smiled gently at the description. A large, well-built young man with a fine sense of humor and flair for the finer things in life, Porky had gained his nickname because of his ebullient self-confidence. To be honest, Porky was quite content with the propaganda of the movies and television. It obviously made it much easier to gather information when the people speaking in his presence were constantly looking over their shoulders for small cringing men with frayed cuffs and terminal coughs, and not paying the slightest attention to the well-dressed, self-confident people in the area.

At the moment, Porky was not working. Or, one might better say, he was engaged in one of his lesser income-producing pursuits. He stood, thoughtfully chalking a pool cue, at the nine-foot, professional table in Sawicki's Pool Hall, carefully considering the plethora of goodies left him by an inadvertent miscue on the part of his opponent, none other than Sawicki himself. The proprietor of the pool emporium, his face twisted in understandable pain as he foresaw the inevitable result of his error, leaned back against the nearby cigar counter, his head and shoulders shadowed in the darkness that lay beyond the cones of light cast by the twin shades, and waited for total disaster. Porky, satisfied that the campaign he had planned would result in clearing the table, leaving himself a proper break shot, and reducing Sawicki's profit for the week considerably, put aside the chalk and bent down, prepared to begin the mayhem. But before he could begin his stroke, the telephone rang. Porky straightened up again politely as Sawicki put down his cue and went to answer the phone. It was not that Sawicki had the slightest doubt, Porky knew, of what was going to happen, but it was simply safer, in that milieu, to have witnesses to the feat—particularly the man who was going to have to pay.

At the telephone behind the counter, Sawicki spat carefully into a spittoon by way of preparation, raised the receiver, and growled into it in his normal foggy voice, "Sawicki's Pool Hall."

"Is Porky Frank there?"

Sawicki covered the mouthpiece with a hand the size of a pool rack and spoke in a conspiratorial whisper that carried the length of the room, disturbing players at several distant tables. "Hey, Porky—you in?"

"Who is it?"

"Same guy calls you here every now and then. Calls you Frank. Quiet voice. Usually sounds tired."

"Ah!" Porky said. He laid aside his cue and moved toward the telephone. "Well, these people who keep silly hours—like nine to five—come the wee hours of the morning and they're all through. No stamina," Porky said sadly, and took the telephone from Sawicki's hand. "Hello?"

"Porky?"

"I suspected it was you, Mr. R," Porky said, pleased with his deductive powers. "Tell me, in confidence, why would a recently married man climb out of a warm bed at this hour of the morning —or any other hour, as far as that goes—"

"I'm not married," Reardon said shortly. "Look, Porky, I have to—"

"Not married?" Porky was properly shocked. "I sat right next to you in Marty's Oyster House less than three weeks ago and heard you propose to a lovely young lady. And I heard her accept. Tahoe was mentioned, object matrimony. And now you tell me you're not married? I shall be a witness. In fact, I'll offer the services of my lawyer—"

"I don't need any lawyers. Porky, I have to—"

"Not for you! You, sir, are a cad! I meant the lawyer for the young lady. I shall suggest she sue for breach of promise, malfeasance in office, contributing to the delinquency of a major— unless the young lady had made colonel by this time, of course—"

"Porky, shut up! Can you talk?"

Porky was far from intimidated by the other's tone; still, he glanced about. Sawicki had tactfully retreated to the pool table, where he gazed upon the spread with anguish, but other ears were in evidence in the smoke-filled room.

"I can speak of ships and shoes, and pool cues, and dollar bills with wings," Porky said cautiously, "but nothing of greater delicacy, I fear. Why?"

"Because if you can't talk, I want to see you someplace else, right away. What places are open at this hour?"

"Now? You want to see me now?" Porky stared in horror back toward the pool table, with the balls laid out there for the easy seduction of his cue. "Right now?"

23

"*Right* now. Where can we meet? What's open at this hour?"

"Other than Sawicki's Pool Hall, I gather you mean," Porky said sadly, and sighed at the vicissitudes of an unkindly fate. "You sure you couldn't wait half an hour . . . ?" He sighed. "No, I suppose not. Well, the Mouse Trap's open and relatively safe, if you don't try their drinks; and there's always Tommy's Joynt—"

Reardon suddenly remembered he hadn't eaten for hours. "Tommy's Joynt in fifteen minutes," he said abruptly, and hung up.

Porky put the receiver back on its hook, stared at the instrument a moment, and then walked dispiritedly back to the table. Sawicki was watching him curiously.

"Sawicki," Porky said, reaching over to retrieve his stick and beginning to dismantle it, "if anybody drives up in a dog sled and asks you, you have my permission to reveal that you're luckier than a guy with two straight cues."

"Hey!" Sawicki said in his gravel voice, unable to believe his good fortune. "Hey, hey! You quittin'?"

"A call from my dying mother's bedside," Porky said dolorously, "and the only thing in this world that could prevent me from putting you into instant bankruptcy." He slid the two halves of his stick into their case and placed the case in his locker. He twisted the combination lock, and moved toward the door. "Remember me in your will," he said, pausing with his hand on the knob. "It's the least you can do."

"Yeah," Sawicki said. He paused and then figured he might as well try it. "But what about the charge for the table?"

Porky stopped and looked the big man in the eye.

"I was only askin'," Sawicki said defensively, and started to rack the balls again to avoid that baleful look. Porky shook his head unbelievingly at the ingratitude of man to man, sighed, and walked out.

Saturday—1:55 A.M.

Lieutenant Reardon was in the act of biting into a large hot roast beef sandwich, a stein of foaming ale at his elbow, when Porky

24

Frank arrived at Tommy's Joynt. Porky waited until the counter-man had provided him with a tuna-salad sandwich, carried it to the bar, where he received a flagon of ale, and brought his booty to the last table under the small deserted balcony, where he joined the stocky detective. The table had been well chosen; at that hour especially it assured as much privacy as could ever be assured at Tommy's. Porky placed his burden on the table, sat, drew a bowl of pickles over more from habit than from need, neatly tucked a paper napkin into his collar, and picked up his sandwich.

"Tuna salad is getting hard to come by," he advised Reardon, apropos of nothing at all. "According to *Consumer Reports*, they're running out of bat wings and mice hair so essential to the manufacturing process." He bit into the sandwich, chewing slowly, his eyes calmly studying the lieutenant across the table.

Reardon took another bite of his sandwich, chewed a moment, swallowed, and edged his beer closer. "There's been a kidnapping," he said quietly.

Porky's face froze slightly, but other than that he betrayed little emotion. There was a slight stiffening of his fingers as he lowered the sandwich. It was not that Porky was without emotion; it was simply that the expression of emotion was a habit he had spent years learning to avoid. It did not fit in with his various businesses.

"That's a nasty word," he said, equally quietly.

"Pop Holland. Mike Holland," Reardon added, and watched the other man's face.

Porky frowned. "Pop Holland? Mike Holland? Am I supposed to know him?"

"Maybe not," Reardon said. "Probably not. He's a cop. Retired today—yesterday, to be exact. A sergeant on Communications these past twelve, fifteen years, I guess. Used to be in Homicide, before I was on the force. A widower. A nice guy. A real nice guy. Sixty-five years old last week. No kids. No family, I gather."

Porky's frown deepened. Anything bad happening to cops often meant a general tightening up of the town, from the hustlers in North Beach to the innocent bookies, wherever they might be. But that, of course, had nothing to do with the case, and certainly nothing to do with the reason Reardon had wanted to meet with him. He drew his ale to him and took a large draught as he thought. He set the flagon down, wiped his lips, and gave his full attention to the problem.

"A retired cop? Any money?"

"None that anyone knows of."

"Any that somebody maybe thinks they know of?"

"I doubt it."

"Any enemies?"

"You don't kidnap enemies; you shoot them, or stab them, or run them over with a milk wagon," Reardon said shortly. "Kidnapping is to punish someone else—financially, usually—but not the victim. It's true the victim often gets killed, but that's generally secondary to the kidnapping itself."

"Then why was he snatched?"

"Now, that's a real good question," Reardon said sarcastically. He shoved his beer glass around the table, staring at the damp trails the glass left. He looked up. "The man said there would be a tape in the mail tomorrow with their demands, addressed to me. Maybe we'll know more, then." He looked at his glass again, avoiding Porky's eyes. "In the meantime, have you heard anything?"

"About a snatch? Or even a potential snatch?" Porky's eyes suddenly narrowed. When he continued there was an edge to his normally pleasant voice. "Mr. R, I hope I am misunderstanding you. True, I usually sell my wares after-the-fact, so to speak, but I sincerely hope you aren't sitting there and suggesting that I would hear anything about a kidnapping—any kidnapping, not just the kidnapping of a policeman—and fail to inform you."

"I didn't mean that at all," Reardon said wearily, and suddenly found himself yawning. He brought the monstrous yawn under control, realizing he was tired, and added a bit lamely, "I just thought you might have heard something in one context, for example, and that maybe you didn't connect it up, but now that you know there's been a kidnapping, maybe—"

"You're getting yourself in deeper," Porky said sternly, but his previous honest umbrage had largely disappeared. "You're tired, Mr. R. You need rest. But I understand what you mean. And, no,

26

I haven't heard a thing." He paused, and then added, "And before you can say it, yes, I shall listen closely from now on."

"That's all I was trying to say," Reardon said, and yawned again.

"That's what I thought was all you were trying to say," Porky said forgivingly, and pushed aside his half-eaten tuna-salad sandwich, looking at it with a curious frown. "You know, they're not as short on bat wings and mice hair as they think, or else they've developed some marvelous substitutes." He drank the last of his ale, dabbed at his lips neatly, and tucked his napkin into his ale mug. He shoved the whole affair away from him and lit a cigarette, prepared to get down to business. "All right. Where did this snatch take place? And when?"

"We think it took place outside his house, in the driveway, late this afternoon," Reardon said quietly. "I was out there with Dondero a while ago, and we got inside the house. Nothing there to indicate nothing; everything looked the way it usually did, I suppose. I was never there before. As for the time, Pop was due at a dinner we were throwing him for his retirement, and he never showed up. In his bedroom there was the stiff cardboard you get with a new shirt, and pins, from the cuffs, you know—"

"Or just to stab you," Porky interjected, but he was listening closely.

Reardon paid him no attention.

"They were on top of the bedspread, so we gather he came home from the Hall, changed clothes, went outside, and that's when they picked him up. His car is gone, so of course they might have snatched him any time after he left the house, but it would be a lot easier to grab him there, before he got started, than it would be after he was in town, with the lights and the people around and everything."

"He might have put on the new shirt this morning."

"Doubtful," Reardon said. "He told the boys he was going home to clean up before the dinner. And his evening paper was in the house, and he's the only one who could have brought it in." He shook his head. "No, the chances are they picked him up when he came out to get into the car. That would be the easiest deal. No neighbor home on the side of the driveway, and it's pretty quiet out there. That's when I figure they pulled it."

"They?"

"They, he, them, or her for all I know," Reardon said wearily. "Anyway, we were waiting for Pop to show up for the dinner, and I got this call. We were at Marty's, in the back room—"

He recounted the events of the evening, beginning with the call from the kidnapper, while Porky listened intently. When Reardon had finished, surprised in his tired state at the amount of detail he had been able to recall—and even more surprised to find himself relating all this to a man in the other's profession—Porky nodded.

"I see. What did this character sound like? High voice? Low voice? Did he sound as if he were trying to disguise his voice? Sound as if he were speaking through cloth, or with a wad of something in his cheek? Although all that does," Porky said in all honesty, "is make you sound like yourself, only muffled." He thought a moment. "You know, I'll bet if you clench your jaw real tight, and then start to choke yourself, you could actually change your voice considerably. You could also, of course, fracture your larynx if you weren't careful, or if you got carried away, but that would be the chance you'd take."

Reardon started to smile and found it turning into a yawn. He tried to remember the nuances of the voice on the phone.

"He sounded—well, educated, but not overly educated, if you know what I mean. He wasn't a dese, dem, and dose guy, but he wasn't the head of the speech department at Berkeley, either. His tone? Medium, I'd say, not deep and not tenor. A little above middle baritone, I suppose you could call it."

"Great. That brings it down to about ninety-nine per cent of the male population."

"I know, but that's the way it is. And he didn't make any attempt to conceal or disguise his voice. He spoke clearly and with no long pauses. And one more thing," Reardon said. He didn't know what made him say it, but suddenly he knew he was right. "Speaking of voices, Mike was in pain when they taped that bit of him talking."

28

Porky looked at him. "In pain?"

"That's right." Reardon waved a hand. "Oh, I don't mean he said 'ouch' or anything like that, but I'm sure they hurt him somewhere along the line. He sounded—I don't know—strained . . ."

"Well," Porky said reasonably, "a man gets picked up and kidnapped on an empty stomach—although if he missed a dinner in the back room of Marty's, that's nothing to complain about—he'd sound a bit strained, don't you think?"

"This was something different," Reardon said stubbornly. He ran his fingers through his hair without being conscious of doing so. "We hear it in the voices of men we see who are shot, or stabbed, or in a bad accident. Before they've been taken care of, while they're waiting for the ambulance, for example. They can be talking about anything else in the world, how it happened, how it wasn't their fault, anything—but underneath their tone is something that says they know they've been hurt, and one part of their brain hangs onto that fact while the rest comes out as usual. Or tries to."

"I'll take your word for it," Porky said, and rapped the table with one knuckle piously, scattering ashes from his cigarette. He brushed them away. "May my own tones remain pear-shaped and pain-free! But, to get back to business, how does the tone of Mike Holland's voice on a tape help to identify the man you spoke to on the telephone?"

"I don't know. What I'm trying to say is I have a feeling the guy was getting a kick out of playing that tape, and the reason he was getting a kick out of it was precisely *because* Mike was in pain when they taped it, if you know what I mean."

"You mean the guy was a mean bastard," Porky said quietly.

"Yeah," Reardon said, and wondered why he had pushed the matter. "I guess that's what I mean."

"Well, it was a good assumption he wasn't an angel to begin with," Porky said logically.

"I suppose so," Reardon said, and yawned. He finished up with a shudder and glanced at his watch. "Well, that's about it, I guess. Keep your ears open. My guess is there'll be a pretty good reward for any information leading to the et cetera, et cetera." He yawned again and shook his head. "I'm about ready to fall asleep on my feet."

"In a moment," Porky said. "Let's see if we can't make us a few assumptions before we break up for the evening." His tone indicated that if he couldn't take a young fortune from Sawicki shooting pool, but had to devote his energies to detecting instead, he might as well do a proper job of it. He brushed ash from his cigarette and leaned back, one hand fondling his empty ale mug. "One—whoever spoke to you on the telephone knew the dinner was being held at Marty's. How?"

"It wasn't any secret."

Porky shook his head, unimpressed by the argument.

"It isn't any secret that Molly's Future can't run in mud for a damn, but I know lots of people who don't know it. Or I hope they don't know it. For instance, I didn't know you were running the dinner, or I'd have asked for an invite." Porky drummed his fingers on the table, thinking. "He also knew about the dinner far enough ahead of time to check out the place and find out they only had the one telephone. Did you know that? I didn't, and I eat there about as often as you do. Item three—or is it two? No matter—he also knew you were in charge of the affair, but he had never met you in person—"

Reardon's eyebrows went up. "Sherlock Holmes stuff?"

Porky waved it away. "You're tired, Mr. R. If he'd have met you, or even spoken to you in person at some time, it's doubtful he would have called you direct. Why take a chance you might recognize his voice? All he had to do was speak with someone else. Right?"

Reardon thought, not for the first time, that Porky Frank would have made a very fine police officer in the Detective branch. He also thought, again not for the first time, that Porky Frank would have been vastly amused at the concept.

"Right. Still, the affair was scarcely a secret. The newspapers even mentioned it."

Porky's eyebrows rose in respect. "The newspapers?"

30

"Well, at least the man who writes the 'View from Nob Hill' column in the *Express*, whoever he is."

"Doesn't he have a name?"

"If he does, he doesn't use it to sign his column. Anyway, he had a big spread about how here we are, the good citizens of San Francisco, with insufficient police protection as it is; and there they are, the police, screaming for more money all the time, just to feed their wee ones; but still we cops can afford to waste our time and money on a retirement dinner for a cop who should be made to work, instead of being put out to pasture when he's capable of doing a day's work, and not allowed to feed at the public trough, et cetera, et cetera. A typical anti-cop blast. You know the sort of thing."

"You seemed to have memorized it by heart," Porky said shrewdly. "Did he mention you by name? He must have."

"He did. He said that people like Lieutenant James Reardon ought to be doing some useful work on the many unsolved murders in our town, work for which he's overpaid, instead of chasing around to restaurants, comparing menus and prices, and tasting the soup to make sure nobody left out the salt."

Porky grinned. "The man has a point. Did you speak with him in person?"

"No, his secretary called. But the column didn't mean anything. As a matter of fact, there was an editorial in the same issue that practically disagreed with everything the columnist said." Reardon shrugged. "It didn't bother me. You know newspapers."

"Fortunately," Porky said, "I don't. Anyway, that sort of publicity doesn't sound like bait for any kidnapper unless, of course, they mean to hold this Holland for the gold watch I assume you meant to give him. Anyway, don't worry about it. Who reads the newspapers?"

"I'm not worried, and lots of people read newspapers," Reardon said, and smiled. "If you don't read the papers, how are you going to know when World War Three starts?"

"If W.W. Three isn't running in the fourth at Aqueduct," Porky said loftily, "it's going to miss me. Which is more than I'm going to do for it." He settled back. "All right. This dinner was mentioned in this 'View from Nob Hill' column. And the column accused you of soup-detecting. But did he specifically say that you were in charge of arrangements? After all, soup-checking is a chore often left to a minor subordinate on the committee."

Reardon's smile faded. He tried to think. "I don't remember."

"Well," Porky said, "it's easy enough to check on. Since you seem to be an *Express* fan, we'll leave that bit of detection to you. And if your being in charge of the dinner *wasn't* in the article, who else might have known?"

Reardon thought a moment and then realized how ridiculous the question was.

"Well, hell! The whole department knew. I said it wasn't any secret. It was on the bulletin board; they had to send their checks to me. So their families knew, and their kids—"

"And their uncles and their cousins who are numbered in the dozens. Well, maybe. Still, I find it hard to picture everyone sitting around the fireplace of an evening saying to each other, 'Say, did you hear the big news? Mr. R is in charge of the dinner for Mike Holland!'"

Reardon frowned. "Just what point are you trying to make?"

"I'm not trying to make a point. I'm trying to hand you what is known, in detective parlance, as a clue."

Reardon's frown deepened. "You mean you think someone in the department might have . . . ?"

"I don't mean anything of the kind," Porky said sternly. "On the other hand," he added, thinking about it, "I don't rule it out, either. Cops have been known to be naughty before. But in this case I honestly don't see a cop snatching another cop. If Holland had forty years on the force, he'd have recognized the man, and some of that would have come out in that tape. No, let's scratch cops."

"Thank you."

"You're welcome. However, let us go on. You say the man on the telephone told you you would receive a tape in the mail tomorrow morning with further instructions. Right?"

32

"Demands, he said."

"Same thing. But," Porky said quietly, fixing Reardon with a steady look, "in that case he must have *mailed the tape* even before he picked up your good sergeant."

Reardon stared. "What do you mean?"

"I mean," Porky said calmly, "let's face the dismal facts about the U.S. mails. This Mike Holland was snatched, according to you, either late in the afternoon or early in the evening. After delivery of the afternoon paper, at any rate. Correct?"

"That's right."

"And the taping of Sergeant Holland's pain-filled voice had to be even later than that, right?"

"Obviously."

"Well, let me ask you a question. Since when have you been able to mail a package—or a letter, for that matter—late one evening and have it delivered in the next morning's mail? Or even the next afternoon's mail? Probably not since 1930, if you want an honest answer. If then. Certainly not today."

Reardon shook his head at his own stupidity. Porky was completely right.

"So where does that leave us?"

"I don't know where it leaves you," Porky said, "but it leaves me with the distinct idea that all packages being delivered tomorrow at the Hall of Justice addressed to you ought to get a more-than-usual consideration. Together with their bearers, of course."

He shot one of his neatly linked cuffs and glanced at the wafer-thin gold watch that was revealed.

"Well, time marches on, to coin a phrase, and you look more tired by the moment. In any event, that's about all the clues I can offer at the moment. I suggest you write them down."

Reardon smiled. "Too tired."

"A minor difficulty," Porky said. He took a thin gold pen from his pocket, wrote "Newspaper" and "Mailman" on the corner of a napkin, tore it off, and leaned across the table, tucking it into the breast pocket of Reardon's jacket. "When you get home, put this under the pillow, and the Napkin Fairy may give you the solution before morning. And do not feel badly that the clues I revealed were not spotted by you. After all," he said in a kindly tone, "you're tired, and this is the shank of the evening for me."

"And where are you going now?"

"I go to listen, as per instructions, *mon Capitaine*—I wonder how you say Lieutenant?—and not, unfortunately, back to Sawicki's," Porky said sadly, and sighed at the memory of that open table.

Saturday—2:50 A.M.

Lieutenant Reardon pulled his Charger into an empty space before the rococo Victorian edifice on the corner of Chestnut and Hyde that contained, among other equally spartan warrens, his own bachelor quarters. He was too weary even to be amazed that a parking space was available practically before his door; most times he was sure the residents of El Cerrito came all the way over here to park, simply to deny him the space. When in a more charitable mood he conceded their real reason was there was no space available nearer.

He swung the wheels to the curb, locked the emergency brake to its fullest—all standard precautions of any San Franciscan who did not want to wake up in the morning and find his car in the bay below—and climbed out, locking the car door. He struggled up the few feet of the steep incline to the worn wooden steps of his building, and regained his balance there, staring up at the house, wondering why he didn't simply lie down on the stoop instead of climbing those mountainous stairs to his own aerie somewhere above. Still, sleeping on the stoop with his normal thrashing about meant taking the chance of ending up in the bay himself, and the thought of waking up under water was distasteful. Besides, he had to get up too early in the morning to waste time rolling down hills.

He let himself into the house with his key and wearily climbed the inside flight to his own personal portion of the ornate old mansion, his footsteps dragging on the worn carpeting, his eyes half closed. He let himself into his living room, switched on the lamp and closed the door, grateful for the silence. Almost three o'clock, which still left four lovely hours of slumber before having to get up and face the hectic meetings that were certain to mark the morning. Four wonderful hours of rest and relaxation before the holocaust! Not the longest time span in the world, but still the equivalent of almost twenty-four ten-minute naps. Why, the thought was practically sybaritic! Four beautiful, wonderful hours! God, a lifetime!

He allowed his jacket to drop unheeded from his shoulders; his necktie was dragged over his head and tossed somewhere in the general direction of a corner. His shoes were scraped off, his trousers allowed to collapse in a pile, his shirt permitted to lie where it fell. The lamp was switched off and he padded toward the bedroom in the dark. Pajamas and toothbrushes were all right in their place, but their place was not here and now; the shade of his mother might scold and threaten eventual dentures, but at the moment sleep was more important.

The mattress felt wonderful as he sank down upon it. He swung his tired legs onto the bed, welcoming the comfort, pulled the covers to his chin, and rolled over, nestling comfortably against the warm figure lying there. "Good night, dear," he murmured absently under his breath, and allowed himself to relax, his mind automatically seeking a means to avoid the problem of Mike Holland's kidnapping, looking for a line of concentration that would lead to soporific release. The answer, he decided, would lie in mentally replaying the front nine of the San Francisco Golf Club course; he usually managed to be sound asleep before he came up to the fifth tee, assuming he didn't get buried in that trap on the fairway leading up to the fourth green—

He sat up in bed abruptly, reached up to turn on the light, and stared down in surprise at the pert little face looking up at him demurely from the pillow.

"Jan!"

"Hello, darling."

"What are you doing here?"

"Waiting for you, dear. You look tired." Jan smiled at him tenderly. "Get some rest. We'll talk about it in the morning."

"But . . ." Reardon fumbled with words. "Does this mean you've changed your mind about getting married?"

"In the morning, darling. Go to sleep."

"But . . ."

"In the morning."

"All right," Reardon said, not quite sure. "If you say so." He lay back again, reached up and switched off the light. So he'd get up at six-thirty instead of seven—what the hell! The night was practically shot, anyway, and it would still be the equivalent of twenty-two or twenty-three ten-minute naps. He smiled at the thought in the darkness and reached out to put his arm around a warm and soft Jan as he drifted off to sleep.

CHAPTER 4

Saturday—8:00 A.M.

The men sitting around the conference room on the fifth floor of the Hall of Justice, waiting for Chief Boynton to arrive, represented the major departments of the Police Department, with both the division head and his chief assistant present. The men had been called in from many endeavors, some from time off, some from duty, some from sleep, but they were all there. Lieutenant Reardon, seated beside the head of Homicide, Captain Tower, leaned back and took advantage of the delay to relive the lovely reunion he had unfortunately been forced to leave such a brief time before.

Jan! How had he ever been lucky enough to find himself a girl like Jan? It wasn't just that she was rapidly becoming known as one of the best of the rising crop of young architects in town; it wasn't just that despite the considerable difference in their education she actually made him feel smart at times; it wasn't even her wonderful looks, with the short boyish hair topping off that lovely face, and the whole kissable head topping off that incredible body; it was—well, he didn't know exactly what it was, but he promised himself he would never again jeopardize their relationship by insisting on marriage if Jan didn't want to marry a cop. When he was really honest about it, he didn't blame her.

Just suppose, for instance, that Kate Holland was still alive; picture her at this moment, sitting home, wondering what some nut was doing to her husband, wondering is she'd ever see him alive again. . . .

The door opened, breaking into his reverie. Captain Clark, of Traffic, was in the doorway. Reardon put aside any further thoughts of Jan; to think of his lovely Jan while looking at Clark's sour bulldog face, with its usual expression of belligerence, somehow didn't seem fitting. Clark looked around the room.

"Nothing on the so-called missing car," he announced to nobody in particular, and dragged a chair around to face Tower. He sat down and stared at the head of Homicide. "That's if the thing is missing in the first place."

Tower frowned. "What's that supposed to mean?"

"Just what I said," Clark said, his chin thrust out. He was looking at Tower but his words were obviously intended for the lieutenant at Tower's elbow. "Mike Holland went out on a toot to celebrate his retirement, forgot all about the dinner you people were throwing for him until it was too late, and then, when he finally remembered, he didn't have the guts to call himself, so he got a pal to do it for him." He shrugged. "And the pal thought he had a sense of humor—"

"So where's his car?" Reardon demanded.

Clark disregarded him.

"When Mike sobers up sometime today, he'll call up or show up all embarrassed, and in the meantime we'll have wasted the time of dozens of men, and put God knows how many patrol cars out of service—"

"So where's his car?" Reardon repeated.

"How the hell do I know where a drunk stashes his car?" Clark said angrily. He snorted. "This town has a million bars and nine tenths of them have parking lots!"

"No way," Reardon said stubbornly. "The footmen have been checking parking lots. Anyway, Mike was sober on that tape. I heard it. It was no gag." He remembered something else. "And he was in pain. I could tell by his tone of voice, even if he didn't say anything."

38

Clark looked at the ceiling in supplication. "Even if he didn't say anything!"

Gentry cut in quickly. Roy Gentry was the head of Laboratory Services and probably knew more about drunks than any other man in the room. The result of the bag tests ended up in his lap, and any blood or urine analyses for alcohol were part of his responsibilities. Gentry was also a conciliator by nature, possibly because he was tall and thin and craggy, and in college somebody had told him he looked like the young Lincoln. If so, it was a Lincoln with spectacles that always appeared to be on the verge of falling from the large thin nose.

"Captain Clark might have a point," he said in what he obviously hoped was a compromising manner. "I would judge it rather hard to determine if a man is drunk or sober merely by listening to a tape recording of his voice. Oh, of course," he went on in a manner that surprised no one in the room, "if he was *really* drunk, where his speech was visibly—I mean, well—where it could be heard to be. . . ." He trailed off.

"Anyway," Clark said, as if he wanted to make clear he neither needed nor wanted Gentry's half-hearted support, "how do we know when that tape was recorded?"

"You mean, Mike Holland might have made a recording ahead of time, saying he was kidnapped? On the offhand chance he might have a few drinks too many on the night of his retirement dinner and forget to show up?" Reardon stared at Clark. "What goddamn kind of sense is that supposed to make?"

"Now, let's not get excited—" Captain Tower began.

"Let's not get excited?" Reardon turned to look at his superior in astonishment. "A cop is kidnapped—*kidnapped!*—and everybody here talks as if the whole thing was a gag of some sort! What do you mean, let's not get excited? I figure on getting *goddamn* excited!"

"Nobody is talking as if it's a gag," Captain Tower began, but this time it was Clark who interrupted.

"Let him get as excited as he wants," he said in a half-amused tone. He turned to Reardon. "Just answer me one question, Lieutenant—who in God's name would want to kidnap Mike

Holland? Why? What would anyone gain? The man has no family, and if he had any money other than his paycheck, I don't know about it, for one."

There was a moment's silence. Then Reardon said quietly, "Damned if I know. But we'll know when that tape comes."

"*If* it comes," Clark began, and then stopped short as the door opened again and Chief of Police Alex Boynton strode in in his usual hurried manner. Boynton had only been promoted a short time, but the change had been one that the huge majority of the men at the Hall favored. He walked to the head of the long table, looked about in the silence that had fallen, and then nodded abruptly, sitting down.

"All right, gentlemen," he said in his deep voice. "Let's get started. Who's first?"

Clark spoke up. "I was saying, Chief, that this whole thing sounds to me as if it could be a gag—"

"You didn't hear that tape and I did," Reardon said, and then was rapped to silence by Boynton.

"Let's take it one at a time," Boynton said. "All right, Lieutenant. You were the one who reported it. Let's start with you."

"Yes, sir." Reardon hitched his chair a bit closer to the long conference table and paused to collect his thoughts. Getting excited and talking off the top of one's head might be all right with a man like Captain Clark, but Boynton was a different matter. "Well, sir, as you know, last night we had scheduled a retirement party for Mike Holland, and he didn't show up. We were waiting for him at the restaurant when there was a call for me, and the caller said that Mike had been kidnapped. He played a tape with Mike's voice on it for proof. Mike said something like—he was talking to these men—*Listen, you dumb baboons, I'm a police officer. I'm a cop. Who in the name of sweet Mary and Jesus is going to give a plugged dime for an old cop?* Or words to that effect—"

"A good question," Clark said, and grinned.

Boynton took one look at Clark and the traffic officer subsided, but there was a twinkle in his eye in appreciation for his own wit. Boynton turned back to Reardon.

"Go on."

"Yes, sir. Well, we all know that 'sweet Mary and Jesus' was a favorite phrase of Mike's. And he hadn't been drinking, not a drop, I'd swear it. Anyway, I asked this character on the phone what he wanted, and he said the demands would be on a tape sent here this morning in the first mail, addressed to me. He said—"

"Why you?" Boynton's deep-set eyes were watching Reardon steadily.

"Sir?"

"I said, why would he address the tape to you?"

"I don't know, sir. He knew my name and he knew I was in charge of the dinner. I'm just reporting what the man said. We tried to trace the call, but Marty's Oyster House—the restaurant the affair was being held at, sir—only has the one phone, and the nearest outside phone was a block away and out of order. The man said he'd put it out of order, which means he knew the area pretty well—"

"It also seems to mean he was an amateur," Boynton said.

"Sir?"

"He seemed to do a lot of talking. Unnecessary talking. However."

"Yes, sir." Reardon frowned, recalling something else. "There was something odd about that call, sir. If he had called from his home, or a house, he would have been taking a big chance of having the call traced. But at the same time, I have to doubt he would have made the call from a public booth."

"Why?"

"Because I can't see a kidnapper standing in front of a window in a drugstore, or out in the open at a street booth, playing a tape recorder into a telephone receiver," Reardon said firmly. "Too many people could see him and remember the scene." He shrugged. "Still, we weren't able to trace the call in any event, so I don't expect it makes that much difference."

"On the other hand," Boynton said, voicing his thoughts, "anyone screwy enough to kidnap a retired cop with nothing but his pension could be screwy enough for anything." He looked at Reardon. "Did the man sound—well—unstable?"

Reardon didn't have to think about that one.

"No, sir. He sounded happy, but not slaphappy, if you know what I mean. Not giggly. Just pleased with himself, as if he'd pulled off a good one and was congratulating himself. He laughed a few times, but it was all plenty sane laughter. He was simply enjoying himself."

"Could he have been on anything? High?"

"I don't think so, sir. He sounded sharp. On the ball."

"Any sort of accent to help identify him?"

"You mean, black or white?"

"Or Chicano. Or British. Or French or Chinese. I mean, any accent?"

"White American, I'd say. Almost certainly white American."

"I see." Boynton drummed his thick fingers on the table before him while he thought about it. "Well, black or white, screwy or not, it might not hurt to have the footmen check out the drugstores in their areas to see if anyone remembers someone using a tape recorder in a phone booth at that hour last night." His eyes came up. "Incidentally, what time was it?"

"He hung up at 10:02, sir."

"Right. The street phone booths would be harder to check, unless we give the story to the media and ask them to ask for the public's co-operation. Maybe somebody—"

"We can't do that, sir," Reardon said quickly. "That was one of the things the man said. No publicity. No newspapers. He was definite on that score."

"I see." Boynton didn't sound surprised. He swung around to a man sitting beside him, scribbling in a shorthand notebook. "Mark, make a note. Get it out to the stations for relay to the footmen. Have them check where possible without advertising. Man at a phone—tape recorder. You know what I want." He swung back. "All right, Lieutenant. What else?"

"Well, sir, we—Sergeant Dondero and myself—went out to Mike's house and I got in using a slip card. There was no sign of any disturbance. The evening paper was on the floor near a chair in the living room; Mike had read it and it comes about five-thirty, because we checked this out with the neighbors. There were signs in the bedroom that he'd changed clothes, for the dinner we can only assume, or our guess is he was snatched when he walked out of the house to get into his car. It's a quiet neighborhood, and apparently none of the neighbors heard or saw anything, because we checked them out, both sides of the street, for a block in each direction. We—"

There was a sharp ring of the telephone, and Reardon paused. Boynton reached over and picked it up, grunting into it. A brief moment and he handed it down the table to Reardon. The lieutenant brought the receiver to his ear.

"Yes?"

It was the lobby desk. "You wanted to know when the mail got here, Lieutenant. The mailman's here now."

"Hang onto him!" Reardon said, and came to his feet. He looked at Tower. "Mailman's here," he said shortly. "Dondero's probably still sacked in—he worked late—but Stan Lundahl ought to be in by now. Could you have him meet me in the lobby?" He glanced at Boynton. "Be right back, sir."

Boynton grunted. The last thing Reardon heard as he left the room was Clark's voice, a bit more respectful since he was addressing the chief, but still the same niggling whine.

"Chief, if you want my opinion, the whole thing still sounds like a tempest in a—" The closing door ended the sound.

Clark! Reardon thought and wrinkled his nose in distaste as he rang for the elevator. If they had to kidnap somebody from the Police Department, why couldn't it have been a loud mouth like Clark? Then none of them would have to sweat getting him free; the kidnappers would undoubtedly throw the bastard out into the street just to stop hearing that voice.

Saturday—8:50 A.M.

Alfred L. Kavulich, Postman, stood firmly beside the wide lobby counter, his expression clearly indicating righteous indignation, his one hand tightly gripping one side of his mailbag, his entire attitude demonstrating his representation of the United States Government, as well as his knowledge of the rights, prerequisites, and responsibilities of such representation. Herodotus may not have included it in his list, but as far as Alfred L. Kavulich was concerned, bag-grabbing was fully as bad as rain, sleet, or dark-of-night any day.

From the other side of the counter, Patrolman William A. Healey, one of three men assigned to day-desk duty, held the opposite side of the mailbag with equal determination, as representing both the people of the municipality of San Francisco and the explicit instructions of Lieutenant James Reardon, which instructions Healey had no intention of disobeying. To Reardon, coming across the marble-floored lobby from the elevators, the touching tableau might have been posed to demonstrate either Devotion to Duty or a test of post office equipment arranged by the Bureau of Standards at the behest of the leather lobby.

He came to the desk, tugged the postman's hand abruptly free of the bag, motioned Patrolman Healey also to relinquish his grip, and without further ado dumped the contents upside down upon the counter. A few letters slid to the floor from the pile. There was a shocked gasp of outrage from Alfred L. Kavulich.

"Hey!" the postman said, voicing his natural resentment at this cavalier treatment of government property, quite as if the destruction of the mail was a privilege reserved for the august members of the postal branch; but Reardon paid the man no attention. He was poking lightly with a closed fountain pen among the several larger brown envelopes and smaller packages that were submerged in the heap. Under his prodding, more letters joined those on the floor, and the postman, torn between calling for the police or picking up the letters, finally realized where he was and bent down. He held the retrieved letters in his hand and glared at Reardon as he straightened up. "Just what do you think you are doing? That's government property!"

"True," Reardon conceded. He had shoved a majority of plain letters to one side and was concentrating on the larger material. "Ah!" He edged one small package free from the pile with the tip of his pen and bent closer to study the face of the package. Healey reached for it but Reardon pushed his hand away. "Don't touch it."

The postman, in the midst of further expostulations, stopped dead. He opened his eyes wider and almost closed his mouth. At last he thought he could see a possible reason for the arrogant

44

treatment that had been accorded both his person and his mail by these madmen.

"What is it? A bomb"

"I sincerely hope not," Reardon said, and considered the postman carefully. Whatever else Alfred L. Kavulich looked like, he didn't look like a kidnapper's accomplice. He touched the package lightly with the tip of the pen. "Where did you pick this up?"

The postman stared. Any doubt he might have had that the entire San Francisco police force had taken leave of their senses, led by the stocky maniac facing him, disappeared.

"Where did I pick it up?" What a question! Where did a postman normally pick up pieces for delivery? At the A&P? "At the post office, naturally! Where else?"

"Without a postmark?" Reardon asked. "Without stamps?"

"What?" The postman looked at the face of the small package and his confusion deepened. "There must be some mistake . . ."

Reardon studied the stunned face a moment. No, Alfred L. Kavulich may have been many things, but a criminal he was not. "That's right," Reardon said quietly. "Who did you meet since you left the post office who gave you this package?"

"Nobody!" On this score Alfred L. Kavulich was ready to wager his life. "Oh, sure, people along the route give me mail to deliver, it's out in the van, not in my bag. And it's got stamps on it; I don't accept mail without stamps. I'd have to—" He suddenly paused, thinking. Reardon waited. "Hey!" Alfred L. Kavulich suddenly said, convinced. "I know! Yeah! It must have been that guy who bumped into me! I thought he was just a drunk, but a nice guy, because even though he dumped my bag, he helped me pick the stuff up." He shook his head dolefully. "And all he was trying to do was to save a couple cents stamps!"

Reardon felt the old familiar tingle of being close to something.

"What did he look like?"

"Like a wino," the postman said, and frowned in an attempt to recall more details. "Yeah, a wino. Drunk. That's why he bumped into me, is what I figured then. Just to save a couple stamps!"

"But what did he look like, damn it?" Reardon was beginning to lose his patience with Alfred L. Kavulich.

"I'm trying to tell you, he was a drunk, a wino," the postman said, aggrieved. "Not staggering, but not all that steady, either. And that breath of his! Wow!" He seemed to realize this scarcely constituted a description. "Let me see—he needed a shave—or maybe he had a beard—I don't remember which. He was a wino, see? You see dozens of them on the street all the time. That's all I can tell you."

Stan Lundahl had come up and was watching with a bright eye. The attitude of Detective First Grade Lundahl was that of a curious bystander; from his exaggerated height he stared down at the pile of mail on the counter with the air of a person who had stumbled on a grab bag in the middle of the street, but was polite enough to wait until asked to particpate. Reardon motioned him closer.

"Stan. This package was added to the mailbag—"

"I heard."

"Good. Then try to find out what the man looked like from this—this—" Words failed him. "From this man. Go back to where it happened. Maybe you'll find a better witness than this—this—" He dropped it. "I want the man who put this package in the mailbag."

"Right," Lundahl said, perfectly agreeable. He tucked a matchstick into his mouth in lieu of the cigarettes he had abandoned in his haste to comply with Captain Tower's order, and turned to the postman. "Let's go. We'll talk on the way."

"But—my mail . . . !"

"So it'll be delivered a little late today, is all," Lundahl said in a kindly tone. "Pretend like it's Christmas. Or any other day, as far as that goes. Nobody's going to steal it; this place is fairly honest, as police stations go. Now, where did this all happen? This bumping and dumping and picking up, and all?"

"Just down the street, practically. I was getting out of my van—"

"And what was the wino wearing?"

"I told you. I—" Alfred L. Kavulich suddenly paused. "He was wearing a windbreaker! Yeah. It was green—"

"A nice Christmasy color," Lundahl said approvingly, and led the way through the heavy glass doors of the Hall to the steps outside, his eyes automatically searching Bryant Street in both directions for a green windbreaker he was sure was far away from there by now.

Saturday—9:10 A.M.

Harry handled the old car with care, his tiny eyes peering brightly from side to side, almost bird-fashion, to see if anyone might be paying undue attention to the car he was driving. The plates had been muddied over, but that still didn't mean it was safe to be driving around with it in broad daylight, even if it was going to be abandoned in a few minutes. And to drive it practically in front of the Hall of Justice, yet! Sure, it was a ten-year-old Chevy like thousands of others, and sure, it was black, like thousands more of others, but still, it belonged to a cop, and a cop that every other cop in the state was undoubtedly searching for at the moment. Crazy! Sure, George wasn't the guy to be afraid of taking chances, but what Harry would have liked to know was, why was it every time George took a chance, it was Harry's neck that was out?

At Harry's side the wino leaned back against the worn upholstery, feeling on top of the world. A grimy hand, jammed into the bottom of the windbreaker pocket, firmly clutched two wrinkled twenty-dollar bills. He could hardly believe his good fortune. Forty bucks just to bump into a postman, dump his bag accidentally-on-purpose, and then help him stuff the junk back in! Plus the little package he had added, of course. He glanced over his shoulder at the small driver with the zoot-suit hat and wondered if maybe he could do other little jobs for the tiny man sometimes. Forty bucks bought a lot of juice. As a matter of fact, with forty bucks a guy could take a step up the ladder and maybe get himself some cheap brandy. It didn't last as long, of course, but it packed a greater wallop, a deeper euphoria. But of course it wouldn't be smart to be sudden-rich and spend it all at once, either. He sighed. Money brought problems, there was no doubt. The thing to do, obviously, was to get a bottle of muscatel and consider the spending of the forty bucks in depth. Or should it be a bottle of cheap brandy?

He looked through the windshield, and was brought from his

dreams of alcoholic grandeur by a slight braking of the car. He frowned as he noticed for the first time where they were. This was miles from where he thought he was being taken; this was a section of town he didn't even know. In fact, from the deserted looks of the area, it appeared that very few people knew it.

"Hey," he said, not complaining especially, since the little man seemed to be a potential source of income to be nurtured, "what are we doin' way over here? I thought you was goin' to drop me where you picked me up. Remember? Down at—"

"You didn't hear good," the little man said quietly. "They'd find you in five minutes down there, and then what? Dumping a mailman's bag is a federal offense. You could get ten years."

"Hey!" the wino said, startled. "You didn't say nothin' like that! You didn't say *nothin'* like that! You said it was a gag, a joke, is what you said. You said they wasn't nothin' to worry about!"

"And there isn't," Harry said evenly. "Not up here. Why do you think I'm dropping you off up here?"

"Yeah, but . . ." the wino began, doubtfully.

"I'm telling you. You drop off here, you've got nothing to worry about. Nobody'll think to look for you up here."

"Oh. Well, okay," the wino said. Anyways, what difference did it make, down there, up here, wherever? Besides, who was going to raise a fuss about bumping into a mailman, anyways? It could have been an accident; who was going to prove it wasn't?

Harry completed braking the car and drew it to the curb. He leaned past the wino, wincing a bit as the stale breath hit him, and pulled down on the door handle. The door swung open.

"Here you are."

"Yeah," the man said vaguely, and climbed out. He hesitated a moment, his hand on the open door, trying to remember what it was he had been thinking about before. Then it came to him and he bent down, peering in at Harry. "Hey, you ever get any more jobs like that, I'm your boy. On'y, how can I get in touch? I don't usually have no fixed place I'm at . . ."

"I'll find you," Harry said confidentially, and leaned over, pulling the door shut.

48

The wino seemed to sense rejection.

"I can help you out in lots of things," he said, trying to interject his words through the slight gap of the almost closed window. "I ain't just good for bumping into people—"

"I'm sure," Harry said, and put the car into gear.

The wino stared down vaguely a moment and then straightened up, looking around. There had to be a bar someplace in the area, even in a deserted neighborhood like this. Hell, where wasn't there a bar in any part of any town in the country? If not this block, the next one. He raised his hand in an uncertain salute to his unknown benefactor and started to cross the street, involved once again in the problem of wine or cheap brandy.

CHAPTER 5

"No fingerprints on the cassette itself, which figures, but we have a lovely bunch from the package," Reardon said. He sounded more sanguine about them than he felt, since the chances were they belonged to the wino who had planted the package. Still, it was a slip-up on the part of the kidnapper, if only a tiny one; first, not to have instructed his messenger about leaving prints, and secondly, using one of the few kinds of paper that retained fingerprints easily. Maybe old happy-voice wasn't as smart as he seemed. "If Stan doesn't pick up the drunk, maybe we'll be able to identify him through the prints."

"If the prints don't belong to the mailman," Clark said dourly.

"The mailman didn't touch that package," Reardon said confidently. "He didn't even know he had it. Anyway, the package and the paper and the string are all down in the lab, on the offhand chance they'll tell us something. In the meantime, let's hear what the tape has to say."

He pulled the tape recorder he had borrowed from the sound lab closer; the men in the room crowded nearer, tense now that the tape was about to be played. Boynton gave a terse nod and Reardon slid the cassette into place and pushed the proper buttons. He stared at the slowly unwinding tape, willing himself a

50

picture of the kidnapper from the voice he was awaiting, a picture that could lead him to the man quickly. Once located, Reardon was fairly sure he could drag some facts from the man, possibly even painfully.

There were several seconds of scratchy silence, followed by a sudden aliveness in the tape, as if it had been slumbering and was now awake and ready to go to work. In the background there was a rhythmic bumping sound, muffled, and then the scratchiness disappeared and the familiar cheery voice broke in on them, too loud. Reardon hastily twisted the knob, the volume dropped until they were straining to hear; he twisted again, bringing the sound to a reasonable level. They apparently had missed little.

"... lo, hello, hello. Testing, one, two, three. Testing, one, two, three. Are you there? Are you ready? No, I'm Reddy's brother. Old joke." There was a break in the voice pattern, during which the strange rhythmic background sound dominated, then even that stopped. Reardon was about to reach for the recorder when the voice returned. "It played back reasonably well, folks. I'd hate to have my deathless prose lost to posterity—or to you folks —simply because I haven't learned how to properly work this ridiculous little gadget, yet. But I'm sure you're not interested in my problems, so let's get down to yours."

There was another brief pause, during which someone in the room was heard to mutter, "He talks too gaddamn much!" Then the voice returned. Now, however, the tone was subtly changed. The lightness still seemed to be there on the surface, but it was only a thin veneer over a deadly purpose. The men around the table stared at the small tape recorder with hard, expressionless faces.

"Gentlemen, we are holding Sergeant Holland as our prisoner, as you know. In order to obtain his release, you will release a prisoner you are now holding in your cell block on the top floor of the Hall of Justice. This prisoner is awaiting trial on a minor charge, and possibly extradition. He means nothing to you, but I want him. His name is Guillermo Lazaretti. You will release this prisoner to us at exactly two o'clock tomorrow morning. You will not be cute and try to follow him once you drop him off at the proper place, nor will you try to put any gizmo on him that might enable you to track him electronically, or any other way. Not that any such gadgetry would work, since we honestly are not fools, but primarily because Sergeant Holland would suffer for any such stupidity on your part.

"Incidentally, I should hate to hear the sound of any helicopter or any low-flying aircraft in the vicinity of the release point, so I suggest you inform the necessary officials of any airports. Two in the morning is scarcely the time for low-flying pleasure craft, so for Sergeant Holland's sake, I hope everyone remembers this point.

"Now, for the release point. Your car, containing just the driver and Lazaretti, will leave the Hall of Justice at precisely one-thirty in the morning. If you wish to keep Lazaretti cuffed during the ride, you may do so, as the cuffs will present no problem, but a third person in the car is strictly prohibited. You will have the driver take Third Street south past China Basin and along the docks. He will pass Central Basin and continue. Just beyond the point where Army Street dead-ends into Third, there is a small bridge that crosses Islais Creek Channel. You will drop your man off at the center of the bridge and immediately drive on and out of sight. And I mean on, and I mean out of sight, and I mean immediately. Nor would I suggest planting anyone either under or even near the bridge beforehand. The only one who would suffer would be Sergeant Holland.

"It's just that simple. Until two o'clock tomorrow morning, then."

There was a stop in the voice recording, although the background thumping sound continued. Reardon stared at the little tle machine as the tape grated on; then the voice was suddenly back and Reardon knew what he had been waiting for. Now the old jollity was back again.

"Oh, yes, I almost forgot, didn't I? If you are all good little boys and do what Papa says, your Sergeant Holland will be freed—relatively unharmed—exactly twenty-four hours later. We haven't decided just where at the moment, but if he needs a dime for a phone call, we'll loan him one. We're not all bad, you know.

"And that, I'm afraid, is really that."

52

This time there was an air of finality about the voice stopping. The background sound returned, fainter now; the tape ran on for several more revolutions and then ended. Reardon leaned over and pressed the STOP button. There were several moments of dead silence in the room; then Captain Tower of Homicide spoke. He sounded puzzled.

"And just who in hell," he asked wonderingly, "is Guillermo Lazaretti?"

There was dead silence as the men at the table all looked at one another in equal bewilderment; then all eyes seemed to turn at the same time to contemplate Lieutenant Zelinski, of Detention.

"Well, Jeez," Zelinski said sullenly. "You know how many guys we got in the tank upstairs? You guys got any idea? What am I supposed to do? Keep track of each one of them individually? Kee-ri!" He reached out a hamlike hand and dragged one of the telephones on the table closer, dialed an internal number, and growled into it when it was answered. He waited and the others waited with him. A moment later Zelinski had the information he wanted and was bobbing his bullet-head up and down as he hung up. "Yeah, now I remember. Sure, now I remember. A foreign guy—"

"We don't extradite many nationals," someone said dryly.

"I remember," Zelinski said, paying no attention to the interruption. "A tough guy. Weighs a hundred pounds dripping wet and because he had a couple weapons on him, he thinks he's Joe Louis. He was picked up in a scrap with another guy, another foreigner, both of them armed. Guns and knives. They were going after each other with the shivs when a plainclothes cop busted it up and called the wagon. Yeah, now I remember. They both come up in front of Judge Melchor either next Wednesday or Thursday, I forget which."

Boynton frowned. "What was all that about extradition?"

"I remember," Zelinski said, as if to flaunt his now-operative memory. "Yeah, now I remember. They both refused lawyers A guy come out from the Italian Consulate. Said something when he left about how they'd both probably be extradited."

"They're wanted in Italy?"

Zelinski grinned. "Naw." His face straightened. "I mean, no, sir. Not that I know of. I guess it's just that the consulate guy figured they wouldn't be wanted over here. I mean, concealed weapons, attempted assault with a deadly weapon—"

"And they're not even citizens," someone said sardonically.

"Yeah," Zelinski said, pleased someone understood.

Chief Boynton brought the meeting back to order.

"Italian eh? The other one, too?"

"Yes, sir. His name is Vito Patrone."

"Were they drunk when they were brought in?"

"No, sir. Sober as a judge, the two of them."

"Did they say what the fight was about?"

"No, sir. Matter of fact," Zelinski said honestly, "neither one of them speaks a word of English, and after we got an interpreter from the courts downstairs, they both clammed up. Haven't said a word since, either one of them."

Boynton drummed his fingers on the table, frowning. "No English, eh?"

"No, sir. Not a word. Or if they have, we don't know it."

"What about their passports?"

"All in order, sir. Tourist visas good for ninety days, issued in Rome a month or so ago."

"Had they ever been in the States before?"

"If they did," Zelinski said, his memory now prodded into working on all twelve cylinders, "it had to be more than four years ago, if they come into the country legally, that is. I remember all about them two guys, now. Yeah. We got their passports upstairs if you want to see them, but I remember them passports. Four years old and no trips to the United States in that time. Other places, I don't remember where, but not here."

"Any other identification on them?"

"Well, their passports, and they each had a wallet and each one had plenty of cash on him, but"—he frowned—"now you mention it, sir, no other I.D. in the wallets." Zelinski had a sudden thought. He pointed toward the tape recorder. "But that guy, he knew Lazaretti, at least by name."

54

"True," Boynton said, not greatly impressed. "What about their passage? Their plane tickets?"

"They didn't have them on them, sir." Zelinski tried to answer what he considered an unspoken criticism. "We figured, what the hell, they'd be out of our hair in three, four days, Chief. We didn't really get very involved with them. They were just in for a street scrap. We get a lot more serious stuff coming through all the time."

If Boynton had been contemplating criticism, he didn't voice it.

"Were they staying in town?"

Zelinski reddened a bit. "Like I said, sir, they didn't hand out any information." He brightened a bit. "But if they were staying in a hotel under their own names—and they probably would be, because maybe they figured they had to turn in their passports here like they do in Europe—it shouldn't be too tough to trace them." A thought came to him. "But we don't have to *trace* them sir. We *got* them."

"Except you say they haven't been overly communicative." Boynton shrugged. "Besides, staying in a hotel without speaking a word of English? My own guess is they'd be with friends or relatives. Not," he added half to himself, "where I can see it makes one damn bit of difference." He drummed his fingers on the table, while he stared off into space, thinking.

Reardon suddenly spoke without really knowing why. Only a faint memory of something Porky Frank had said—or hadn't said, he didn't recall which at the moment—seemed to prompt him.

"Was there anything in the newspapers about these two characters? Being picked up by the police, I mean?"

Zelinski shrugged. "I haven't the faintest idea. If there was, I didn't see it. I can't imagine who would be interested, but there's always reporters hanging around, and one of them maybe might have put in a squib. Easy enough to find out, I suppose. Just ask the reporters."

"Yeah," Reardon said, and fell silent.

Captain Vinocur, of Communications, spoke up. He had been Mike Holland's latest superior, and had been lying back in the

55

bushes, waiting to see what would develop. He was a giant of a man, with spiky black hair that jetted from his wrists and arms, as well as his head, removed to Communications after ten years, eight citations, and three trips to the hospital as head of Narcotics.

"All right," he said in his booming voice. "In the meantime, what do we do about Mike?" He glared around the room. "Damn it, he's a good man!"

"Well, damn it yourself," Clark said with even more than his usual irritation. "We sure as hell don't let ourselves get black-mailed, that's for damned sure!" He seemed to have forgotten that moments before he had been positive the entire thing had been a tempest in a teapot. "Look like bloody idiots if we did!"

"Except that it might make it a little tough on Mike, don't you think?" It was Captain Tower, huge in a suit that seemed, as usual, far too small for him. He spoke in a deceptively mild voice.

There was a brief silence, broken by Chief Boynton.

"Captain Clark has a point," he said. He had forced all emotion from his voice and was speaking in the flat, impersonal tones of a person responsible for the Police Department, and not as an individual. He paused in his finger-drumming and looked at Tower, but he was addressing each man in the room independently, and each man knew it. "Let's face it—if we let one prisoner be exchanged for a kidnapped police officer, there wouldn't be a police officer safe on his beat, or in his patrol car, or in his home, or anywhere else, from then on."

Vinocur started up in his chair, prepared to argue, his big pockmarked face reddening. He was in no mood to watch his language at the moment, chief or no chief.

"Now, let's wait a goddamn second! You mean we just sit around on our big fat duffs and let Mike Holland go down the drain? What the hell gives around here? A couple guys get into an argument on the street, so they get pulled in! So what? So they were armed. Who in hell isn't, in this town, for Christ's sake? Ten-year-old kids got guns in this town! And these two guys, they didn't kill anybody—nobody even got hurt! So we let one of them

56

go in exchange for Mike, for a police officer! What's the difference we let him go or Judge Melchor fines him fifty bucks next Wednesday or Thursday and then kicks his ass out of the country? You tell me, what's the difference? Except maybe Mike gets taken out of the play in the meantime!"

"It's the principle of the thing, dummy . . . !" Clark began, but Boynton cut him off abruptly.

"Let's all calm down. And watch our language." He frowned and began drumming on the table again, speaking in a low voice, as if more to himself than to the meeting. "And it isn't the principle of the thing, at all. Principles are great when they're practical, but otherwise they're just so much shouting down a rain barrel."

He swung around to look Vinocur in the eye.

"Let's keep remembering one thing—the crime here isn't a street fight, where we can make up our mind easily to let a hood go. The crime here is kidnapping. And you ought to know as well as anyone how often the victim of a kidnapping is ever freed after the demands are met. Especially if he's in a position to identify his kidnapper. You know as well as I do that the percentage is that Mike Holland is dead right now, whether you want to face that fact or not."

Vinocur couldn't wait for the chief to finish before he burst out:

"Then what in hell is to be lost by letting this Lazaretti go?" He looked around the table, as if soliciting support. "Anyway, maybe you kill a kidnap victim if big dough is involved, but just to get some two-bit punk out of hock? Why would any guy kill a cop just to get a man out of jail who'll be out in three, four days anyway?"

"I don't know why the man on that tape wants this Lazaretti out right now," Boynton said quietly, "Probably because he may well be extradited to Italy at once, and not be available. But that's not the point. The fact is this man has kidnapped a police officer who can identify him. And you can talk around it all you want, you still know what the chances are for the victim in cases like that."

"Maybe," Vinocur said. He had cooled down somewhat during

the chief's last statement. Then he added a bit desperately, "But on the other hand, sir, maybe Mike's still alive. And even if you're right, like I said before, what's the big loss in letting some small-time punk go just on the tiny chance that maybe Mike is still all right and will be all right? A couple of lousy days in the time of some nobody tough guy—that's all that would be lost." He stared at Boynton. "Maximum."

"It's still the principle of the thing, I say," Clark started.

Boynton cooled him with a look. He turned back to Vinocur, considered the scowling face a moment, and then looked around the circle of frozen faces slowly, pausing a moment at each man's face to consider him individually.

"All right," he said at last, without any expression in his deep voice. "Let's spread this thing around. What do the rest of you think?" He held up a broad palm, interrupting the four or five voices that had instantly broken out. "Wait a second. Before you speak, just remember a few things. One—in the entire history of this world, nobody ever reduced terror by giving in to it. Nobody. Ever. And that's what we'd be doing. Two—a police officer—and for the purpose of this discussion Mike Holland is still a police officer, retired or not—automatically accepts certain risks when he signs up for the job. Among those risks are to do whatever is necessary, at whatever personal risk, to protect innocent people, and this includes his fellow officers. If we give in to this man's demands, I tell you again in my honest opinion, no cop will ever be safe in this town again. Three—this Lazaretti is the only connection we have at the moment with the kidnapper. If we let Lazaretti go, we'll probably be releasing our only chance of ever catching the man who kidnapped Mike Holland. And last but not least—"

He paused a moment before continuing, adding emphasis to his words.

"—if Mike Holland is still alive, the chances are he'll only stay alive as long as this man's demands are *not* met. The minute his demands are met he'll have every reason to eliminate Mike. Remember, kidnapping comes under the Lindbergh law, whether the ransom demanded is a small-time tough guy or a billion dollars." There was another pause; then Boynton said in a quieter tone, "All right, that's how I feel. Now, let's have your opinions."

There was dead silence. Even Vinocur had nothing to say. Boynton sighed.

"All right. Then this Lazaretti stays in his cell, and beyond Wednesday or Thursday, too. Until we get the man who wants him out; until we get Mike Holland"—he did not feel it necessary to repeat the possibility of Holland being dead—"and the man who kidnapped him."

Captain Tower cleared his throat. "Which department gets it?"

"All departments. I'll co-ordinate myself." He turned to Roy Gentry, all business now that the decision had been made. "From the laboratory, the first thing I want is a complete study of that tape. Voice patterns and graphs. Possible places of purchase; all efforts to trace. Call on any department you want for legwork, or hands; call on outside tape experts if you need them. Maybe some of those people who studied the eighteen-minute gap in the Watergate thing, if necessary. Since Lazaretti just came from Italy and hadn't been here before that we know, we'll also want to know if there might be any indication the speaker on the tape could be of Italian extraction, or anything else you can determine. Age, if possible, or education—"

"Also any idea as to what that funny background sound could be," Reardon said, interrupting.

Boynton frowned at the interruption and went back to Gentry.

"Also any ideas on anything. Including the package it came in, string, paper, inside box; everything." He swung around to Clark. "I want Traffic to concentrate on Holland's car. The bridges; maybe the toll-booth attendants will remember something, if he crossed a bridge. All garages, the streets, public parking lots. The car may be parked someplace overtime." His voice turned conversational. "I remember one time we looked all over for a car, damn thing was downstairs in the police garage, pulled in for scofflawing. Everyplace."

He turned to the man at his elbow, still scribbling.

"Mark, I want the stations to have their footmen check out drugstores, public buildings, movie theaters—any places that have interior telephone booths, and see if anyone might have seen a man with a tape recorder in a booth last night. Bus stations, the airport—everywhere. They'll also be keeping their eyes open for Holland's car. What kind was by the way?"

"Black Chevy, four-door sedan," Clark said. "1965. Plate number 6Y-286." Reardon looked across at him in surprise and then shrugged. A bastard he was, but he was still a cop.

"Mark it down," Boynton said. "All of you." He turned to another man, busy scribbling the license number in his notebook. "Dave—"

Davidson, of Robbery, looked up.

"I want your men to go out to Holland's house and go through it with a fine-tooth comb. Not just the top, but under the rugs. Look for a safe, or secret compartments. Look in the cellar. Look for betting slips, or a possible tie-in with gambling—" A hush had fallen on the room. Boynton was aware of it. "I know," he said quietly, "but we do this all the way." He turned back to Davidson. "Also check the driveway and the garage for any hint as to what might have happened. Hit the neighbors again, any enemies Holland might have had we don't know about. And don't stop at one block either side of the house—go two blocks, or three. And check the stores near there, where he bought stuff, the butcher, the liquor stores, the bars. You know what I want."

He turned again. "Sam—"

Captain Tower looked at the chief without expression. "Chief?"

"Well, nobody's been murdered yet in this affair, at least that we know, and I know you've got your hands full . . ." The chief considered a moment. "Well, since your men have started out after the drunk who put the package in the mailman's bag, you might as well continue on that. And then maybe you ought to have a man down at Third at that channel bridge tonight . . ." He paused to think a moment. "No, that's not such a good idea. Let's play it his way, at least for the time being. In fact, Clark, you better tell the patrol cars to steer clear of that area from one to three in the morning, at least."

Clark leaned forward.

"Maybe we could still keep an eye on the bridge, sir. From the water. In fact, I wouldn't be surprised he plans on picking up this Lazaretti by boat—that's why he wanted it at that channel bridge, sir!" The more he thought about the idea the better he liked it. "Yes, sir! We could get hold of the Harbor Patrol—"

"That's an idea," Boynton said, and turned to the man at his side. "Mark, be sure and contact the Harbor Patrol and tell them to keep their goddamn boats away from the Islais Channel Bridge —in fact, tell them to keep the hell away from that whole side of the bay unless the city is burning down. Okay? From one to three in the morning. After that they can go back to fishing for gropers." He gave Clark one look and then turned back to the room in general. "Who do we have who speaks Italian?"

Reardon spoke up quickly.

"Sergeant Dondero, sir." Damned if Homicide was going to be left out of the case altogether! He knew Dondero spoke some Italian—he was positive he swore in it fluently—but he wasn't sure about the normal vocabulary. He only hoped it was enough; it would be a pity to hang Don because of his own big mouth.

"Fine. Well, he can be detached from Homicide, temporarily. I want him to try to check on all the hotels to see if Lazaretti stayed at any of them—Lazaretti or the other one, whatever his name is. I want him to try and find out who Lazaretti was in contact with, what phone calls he got, and so forth and so on. I want him to check with the Italian Consulate, with Interpol, or with anyone else he can think of, to see if he was known. He can try the neigborhood clubs; they're strong in old-country family relationships. Maybe there was a vendetta of some sort." He nodded. "Have him look for any possible connection with the Organization here, although I doubt the Organization would fool with kidnapping a cop. Or that they would tolerate a long-winded joker like that on their payroll. And have him interview the man—"

Captain Tower leaned over to speak quietly into Reardon's ear. "And you stick with Dondero, understand?"

Reardon grinned and then straightened his face. "Yes, sir."

"Good." Tower rolled back.

Boynton turned to Lieutenant Giordano, of the Loft Squad. "Tim—"

He was interrupted by a brief but loud series of rappings on the door, after which it was opened diffidently. Stan Lundahl stuck his head in, looked around until he located Reardon, and then straightened up, holding the door open with one hand. Boynton looked at him severely, not pleased by having his instructions interrupted.

"Is there something you want?"

"Sir, I was looking for—"

Lieutenant Reardon stood up. "It's Detective Lundahl, sir, from our department. He went after that wino." He looked at Lundahl, fearing the worst from the doleful expression on Stan's face. "Well? What happened? Did you find him?"

"Yeah," Lundahl said, to Reardon's surprise. He took a deep breath and went on. "He's downstairs in the morgue. He was run down and killed up in Potrero, out at the end of a dead-end street on top of the hill. No witnesses, at least so far. We found the car that hit him abandoned less than a block away. Frank Wilkins is finishing up with it now; he should have it down in the garage in an hour or so at the most."

He saw the look on Reardon's face and nodded lugubriously.

"Yeah," he said heavily. "Yeah. We also found Mike Holland's car. It did the job. And if they used it to kill one guy, why should they play tippy-toe with Mike . . . ?"

CHAPTER 6

Saturday—11:30 A.M.

Dondero sat with one knee shoved tightly against the edge of his desk, looking at Reardon with a vicious glower. He had his fingers tented and he pressed them together tightly, then suddenly released the pressure, only to repeat the gesture again and again. It looked as if he were practicing isometric exercises and he was, but Reardon knew it was more than that; it was one of the few indications Dondero ever gave of being deeply concerned about something. He finally gave up the finger exercises, flexed his fingers into fists several times, and then slammed one hand down on the desk top with a bang.

"Jeez! So Pop gets thrown to the wolves, huh? Just for some zero character who got picked up in a street fight!"

"With a shiv in his hand and a gun in his kick," Reardon reminded him.

"With a shiv in his hand and a gun in his kick," Dondero repeated disgustedly. "Man, that's rare, that is! Almost as rare in this town as fog!"

Reardon sighed helplessly.

"Look, Don. It was talked over and the decision was made. I've tried to tell you why six times, but you just don't want to listen. Any maybe it was the right decision. I don't know."

"It was talked over! The way you told it, Boynton talked it over with himself, asked himself to vote, and surprise, surprise! Unanimous!" Dondero snorted. "Talked over!"

"Everybody had a chance to speak his piece. Vinocur let go loud and clear."

"With what result?" Reardon remained silent. Dondero nodded. "Yeah. And what was your contribution?"

Reardon reddened.

"Look, let's not waste all day sitting around here discussing it. I want to go up and talk to this Lazaretti with you, and then I want to go over Pop's car down in the garage—" He suddenly paused, frowning. "I told them you speak Italian. Do you?"

"And how would you know if I didn't?" Dondero shoved his swivel chair away from his desk abruptly and came to his feet, jamming his fists angrily into his jacket pockets. "I still say we ought to deliver the bastard and get Pop back; but all right, let's go up and have our little chat. Let's see how good *his* Italian is!"

They walked out of the office and down the wide hallway to the stairwell. The dentention cells were only two floors above them and neither man was in the mood to stand waiting for the elevators. Reardon glanced sideways at Dondero's rigid jaw and then looked away. He could understand the other man's resentment at the decision, but he could also understand the attitude of Chief Boynton. Even though the majority of men in the department knew it was only a fantasy, most of them always had secret dreams of arriving at the exalted position of top man, and now for a moment Reardon honestly wondered if it was worth it. There were a lot of tough decisions to be made up there, and like the man said, if you can't stand the heat, you ought to stay out of the kitchen. Or out of that big fourth-floor office with the Chief of Police medallion on the door.

They shoved through the swinging doors leading from the stairwell to the detention-cell section, paused to unclip their belt holsters and deposit them with the security guard in his cage there, and then waited while the automatic main cell door to the inner prison corridor was activated and slid open.

"Lazaretti," Reardon said to the inside guard.

"Sure, Lieutenant. What's his number?"

"No idea. He's the man only speaks Italian. Brought in for fighting. Or he's one of them, anyway."

"Oh, yeah. I know the one," the guard said. "He's the little guy. You want to see him in his cell, or in the conference room?"

The "conference room" was one of the cells built for recalcitrant prisoners who had to be put into solitary for any one of many reasons. The cot and its hardware had been removed, and only the lidless toilet broke the austerity of its solid-wall interior. It had the advantage of being soundproofed, which offered privacy to both the prisoner and his interrogator during an interview, without the necessity of leaving the cell-block area. Unfortunately, it also had the distinct disadvantage of giving the interrogator the feeling of what solitary confinement at the Hall of Justice was like; and most of them didn't like it.

"Conference room," Dondero said without hesitation, and looked at Reardon as the guard left to get the prisoner. "It might get a little noisy, and there's no sense in disturbing the neighbors."

Reardon frowned. "Now, see here, Don. We don't have a thing on this man, other than the weapons charge and the assault thing. We don't have a thing to connect him with—"

Dondero held up a hand, cutting off the flow of words.

"You look, Jim. I'm quite sure they read him all his rights, probably in two languages, when they booked him, and you know I'd never do anything that wasn't in the book. But what you don't know is that us Italians, see, we get pretty emotional at times, and when I hug him he's liable to start crying for joy—"

He paused as the guard came up leading the prisoner. Lazaretti was a small man with fine delicate features, dressed in a wrinkled suit of Italian silk, with smooth Italian handmade shoes, and with an expensive silk white-on-white shirt that may have been clean at one time, but which showed the effects of being worn for more than four days in a row, even though it was evident an attempt had been made by the prisoner to maintain it as much as possible. Dondero knew the man had been given his choice of clean prison clothes, so he scarcely felt much pity for him. The necktie had been removed, of course, together with the belt and shoelaces, and the absence of the tie made the neck appear even more scrawny. Lazaretti's hair was long, dark, and wavy, and had been cut in the latest style; the days in prison had allowed the edges to become shaggy, but otherwise it was neat. Dondero would have bet a week's pay that when Lazaretti had been searched, they had found in addition to the shiv and the gun, a comb probably treasured more by the prisoner than the weapons. Still, despite the lack of size, there was a look of cold determination on the frozen features.

Dondero's expression remained fixed, but inwardly he was smiling. He knew the type all too well; the small tough guy. They were the kind he liked.

"In here," he said to the prisoner in Italian, and waited with exaggerated politeness until Lazaretti had preceded him into the small confinement cell. Reardon crowded in and closed the door behind them. It was instantly pitch dark. The lieutenant opened the door, switched on the light from outside, and then closed the door after him once again. The fact that now there was light, coming from a small bulb set in the ceiling, made the tiny cell bearable, but just. Reardon leaned back against the door, watching.

"Real cozy," Dondero said in English, and then switched to fluent Italian. Reardon's eyebrows raised in surprise. He didn't understand a word, but the speed and effortlessness of the demonstration impressed him. "All right, friend," Dondero said. "Let's start at the beginning. What brings you to the United States?"

There was silence. The prisoner stared at the wall, only inches from his face, quite as if he had not heard the question. Dondero suddenly raised his hand and slapped the frozen face openhandedly. The long hair flew; the small head bounced against the wall. The little man turned to stare at Dondero with a dazed expression slowly hardening to hate, and then brought up a small hand to rub the side of his head.

Reardon straightened up instantly, reaching out a hand. "Hey, Don!"

"Man's deaf," Dondero said lightly. "You'd be surprised how sometimes something like that clears the ears."

Reardon's jaw tightened. "Look, Don, I don't want to pull rank, but—"

Dondero dropped the light tone, glaring at the lieutenant savagely.

"You don't want to pull rank, then don't! If you've suddenly gotten a weak stomach, why don't you wait for me downstairs? This character has a connection with the goon who's holding Pop Holland, and he's going to tell me what it is, and in great detail, before he walks out of here. *If* he walks out of here!" he added grimly.

"But not that way!"

"Then what way? You wanted me to question him, didn't you? What did you want me to ask him? How you get from Market Street to the Colosseum? His momma's recipe for pizza? Good Christ! There's only one way a character like this is going to answer questions, and that's if he knows he'll be picking his teeth off the floor if he doesn't!" He saw the hard look on Reardon's face and added more quietly, but just as insistently, "Jim, Jim! Listen to what I'm saying! This man has some connection with the guy who's holding Pop. I'm going to get it out of him. Because if you make me leave him alone, I'll just wait until Judge Melchor lets him go in a couple of days and then I'll be a lot rougher with him than I can be here. Here, I'll try not to mark him; outside I'll rip both his arms off and beat him black and blue with the bloody stumps if I have to!" He shrugged. "So take your choice."

He waited a moment. Reardon was silent. Dondero nodded and returned to the prisoner, changing back to Italian.

"A little disagreement between me and my friend. You lost. Now, let's start all over. What brings you to the United States? And silence is not considered an answer."

The small man looked from face to face, apparently read his fate in the expressionless look on the face of the lieutenant and the triumphant glitter in the other detective's face. Then he said, sullenly, "To visit my cousin."

Dondero indicated no particular triumph in having broken the ice, but continued evenly. "Oh? And just where does your cousin live?"

"In New York. In Brooklyn."

"I've got news for you, friend," Dondero said. "You missed Brooklyn by three thousand miles. What I meant to say was, what brings you to California? Specifically, what brings you to San Francisco?"

There was silence. The little man jammed his jaw tight, and then shut his eyes, squeezing them tightly shut as Dondero raised his hand. Reardon bit his lip as Dondero's hand came down, changing direction, and chopped viciously at the small man's stomach.

"No marks, like I said," he said in Italian, probably thinking he was addressing Reardon, or maybe just talking to himself, or even possibly to advise the little man what to expect in the future. He shook the little man until the eyes opened, and then shook him a few more times for luck; the long hair flew. "You must like getting shoved around," Dondero said evenly. "Well, you got the right guy, because I'm willing to work out on you all day long. You'll wish you were home. Now, what brings you to San Francisco?"

The little man massaged his stomach. His face was gray with pain. He stared at Dondero's pleasant look of comradeship a moment and then shivered involuntarily. That look of false friendship was one he had seen before; it was a look he had employed himself in the past when he had the upper hand and was prepared to use his advantage. It was not a good look to see on the face of a tough opponent.

"I—to see it. They all said San Francisco was worth seeing. They said it was beautiful. . . ."

"They did, huh? Who are all these boosters?"

"I beg your pardon?"

"I said, who told you about San Francisco?"

"People in Italy," Lazaretti said vaguely. He saw the hardness that twitched Dondero's jaw and added hastily, "And my cousin in New York. He said so, too."

"Yes," Dondero said, relaxing, "it is, indeed, a beautiful city. Now, how did you manage to enjoy this beautiful city of ours, when hardly anyone you run into on the street happens to speak Italian?"

"Pardon?"

"I said, who was your interpreter?" There was silence. Dondero reached out and took the small man by the arm, slowly tightening his grip on the thin biceps. "Am I speaking too fast for you? Did you understand the question?"

Lazaretti swallowed and said, still in Italian, "I had no interpreter. I—I—you see, I have a little English. . . ."

"You have? Great!" Dondero accommodatingly switched to English. "Then tell me in English, which portion or neighborhood of our delightful metropolis did you particularly relish?"

Lazaretti stared at him, his eyes hopeless. Reardon was sure he could not understand.

"Ah, well, the hell with it," Dondero said, dropping the matter as well as the small man's arm. He went back to Italian. "We're not here to give you lessons in English. We're here to get answers to questions. Let's skip the preliminaries and get down to the nitty-gritty. Who in this town do you know who is so interested in getting you sprung from jail?"

The little man looked up, surprised. Dondero frowned. Either the little character was honestly startled by the question, or he had to be the best actor to come out of the old country since Vittorio De Sica.

"Pardon?"

"You heard me," Dondero said. "Somebody in the town wants you out of jail, and he isn't being subtle about it, either." He frowned and looked at Reardon, returning to English. "Which brings up an interesting question—how come this little monkey isn't out on bail? Or if he couldn't raise it, how come the character who's got Pop Holland didn't spring for the bail and take Tiny Tim, here, home under his arm?"

"He's up for extradition when, as, and if he gets out of here after his trial," Reardon said, surmising. "They seldom set bail for foreigners up for extradition because they probably figure a large number of them wouldn't show up at the dock."

"True," Dondero conceded, and went back to Italian. "Like I was saying, somebody wants you out of jail very badly. Who? Take a guess if you honestly don't know." Dondero had a feeling he was whipping a dead horse, but he had to keep trying. He reached for the small man's arm again and squeezed. "Try talking."

Lazaretti looked bewildered. For the first time he became almost voluble.

"I don't know a soul in this town. Nobody—"

"No? How about your friend? The guy you were trying to carve up with your shiv when you got picked up?"

"He—I—I don't know him. . . ."

"Oh, come on," Dondero said disbelievingly. "You come over on the same plane from Rome, you come out here in the same plane"—it was a guess, but Dondero was suddenly sure—"you leave New York the same day, holding hands, and you don't even know the guy?"

"I—I don't know anyone out here." The prisoner looked up, convinced Dondero had done his worst. "Anyway," he added bluntly, "they cannot hold me for what I did. What did I do? A fight! Americans do not take such things seriously. I will be free very soon."

"Don't hold your breath," Dondero said, and smiled wolfishly.

"What do you mean?" The prisoner thought he might see an answer and it was an answer he did not like. "What did he do? This man, to get me out of prison?" His hands came up expressively, palms out. "I am not responsible! I am not responsible!" He frowned at Dondero. "What did he do, this man?"

"I'll ask the questions. Let's start over. Why are you here in San Francisco?"

"I told you!"

"What did you tell me?"

"I—I came to visit. Just to visit. Many people come to visit, do they not?"

Dondero looked at Reardon. "Jim, don't you have something else to do? This looks like it may take some time."

"Don," Reardon said coldly, "you're going to get in one hell of a jam if you rough up this prisoner. You—"

"You ought to be getting hungry around now," Dondero said, quite as if Reardon had not spoken. He sounded quite concerned.

"Why don't you run down for a sandwich? Or, wait a second—Pop's Chevy ought to be in the garage by now. Didn't you say you wanted to see it as soon as it came in?"

Reardon looked at him a long moment and then sighed.

"All right, Don. Just don't get your butt in a sling. None of these characters are worth it."

"I'll be as careful as a mother with her first-born."

Reardon looked at him and then shook his head. "All right. I'll be down in the garage when you're done. Or back in the office."

"I'll try not to keep you waiting," Dondero said with satisfaction, and turned back to the prisoner as Reardon closed the solid door behind him. Lazaretti stared at the closed door with widening eyes and then turned to stare at Dondero's hard, smiling face.

"Now," Dondero said pleasantly, "where were we?"

Saturday—2:15 P.M.

The sandwich Reardon had sent out for—or, rather, the portion of it he had eaten—lay in his stomach like sautéed concrete; the waxy cardboard taste of the coffee remained with him even though most of the indescribably terrible liquid had been assigned, together with its leaky container, to his wastebasket. The awful excuse for a meal had only one redeeming grace; it made him look forward even more anxiously to whatever restaurant Jan would choose for their evening repast. After which—

He brought his mind back to business and punched the button for the elevator at the fourth floor. As if it had been waiting for him, the doors slid back and he walked in, pressing the button for the basement garage. He rode down in silence, got out at the lower floor, and walked the long distance to the large caged area at one end of the huge underground room, his footsteps echoing hollowly from the concrete floor. The cage was the storage area for the cars awaiting or undergoing inspection from any one of the Accident Prevention Bureau teams. Lieutenant Frank Wilkins, of the APB, was there beside the old Chevrolet, busily taking notes,

71

a cigarette hanging from one lip, its ash dribbling on his lapel. His men were all over the car, calling out their findings; the trunk was open and a man was bent inside carefully passing a hand vacuum cleaner over all surfaces. The side door on the driver's side was also open and a man there was shoving the rear seat cushion back in place; to one side on the floor of the garage were two small, carefully marked bags with material the vacuum cleaner had picked up in both the front and rear seats.

Wilkins looked up from his notebook at Reardon's arrival, dropped his cigarette on the floor, stepped on it, and nodded pleasantly. Lieutenant Wilkins had been Sergeant Wilkins until a few months before, but the change in rank had not changed him in the least. He was a thickset man approaching fifty, with a rather high-pitched voice and a flattened nose that gave his face a permanently sneering look, but which was actually the result of having his face smashed in by a frying pan years before while trying to break up a family fight. The fact was that Frank Wilkins was the mildest and most co-operative of officers, and was also excellent at his job. Reardon smiled at him and glanced at the notebook in Wilkins' hand.

"Anything of interest?"

"Only fingerprints are those of Pop Holland, which we figured anyway. Stuff in the bags will go to the lab; have a better idea about those when we get through," Wilkins said. "Right now we have blood on the top of the front seat, passenger side. My guess is they cut Mike. Maybe he was giving them a hard time, or something."

Reardon looked through the open front car door. The man who had wrestled the back seat cushion back in place was now delicately shaving samples from a brownish stain that covered the top of the front seat back, and which trailed down the seat cover in ragged tailings. As Reardon watched, the man neatly tipped the shavings into an envelope, closed it, and began to write on it. Reardon looked at Wilkins.

"A lot of blood?"

"No. Nowhere near enough to indicate anything serious."

"What about the mileage?"

72

Wilkins frowned. "What about it?"

"I mean—anything to indicate how far he'd gone?" Even as he asked the question he realized how stupid it was.

Wilkins smiled. "You tell me what it was before they picked him up, and I'll give you a rough idea."

Reardon was floundering. "I meant, like if he'd had an oil change lately, maybe they might have marked the mileage. . . ."

Wilkins shrugged and walked around to raise the hood. A stained tag on the air filter gave him the mileage of the last oil change; he walked back and stared in at the odometer, then shook his head.

"A difference of over two thousand miles, and I'm sure they don't have Mike stashed in some dump in Acapulco." He smiled at Reardon. "Really scraping the bottom of the barrel, aren't you, Jim?"

"Just about," Reardon said, and smiled ruefully. He walked to the front of the car and studied the partially dented hood, the bent license plate. "Any doubt that this was the car that killed that wino?"

"None," Wilkins said promptly. "Green suede shreds on the corner of the license plate, some of the victim's hair caught in the channel between the fender and the hood panel—he must have come over the top and slammed into the fender—same paint on the jacket and the skull as the car paint. Not a shadow of a doubt."

"That sounds definite enough." Reardon studied the car and then looked up. "Frank, do you think the car can really tell us anything useful? Anything that would help us trace the bastard who pulled this job?"

Wilkins shrugged. He fished out another cigarette, lit it, and inhaled deeply.

"No idea," he said at last. "I have a hunch everything connected with a crime could tell us a lot more than it does, if we only had the brains to read the signs. Oh, we read some of them, but I often wonder how much we miss. For example"—he waved a hand at the car—"I would make an educated guess that the job was pulled by two men, and the man who was the boss of the operation sat in the back seat while the other man drove. That

73

guess is based on the pattern of the bloodstain on the back of the front seat. If the driver had leaned over from his position back of the wheel to make the cut, the blood would have been more central on the seat cover, but from the blood pattern, I'd say the cut was made from behind. And if the man in the back seat was doing the cutting, then it's an educated guess that he was the boss of the show. Besides," he added, "the driver was a little fellow—approximately five-foot-four—so you'd naturally figure the bigger guy was the boss."

"Unless they were both midgets," Reardon said, and then suddenly realized what he had heard. He stared at Wilkins. "Man, I'm running into a lot of Sherlock Holmes stuff lately! How do you figure the driver's height?"

Wilkins smiled. "Easy. From the setting of the front seat to the wheel; from the placement of the rear-view mirror in relation to the seat; in the angle of the side-view mirror." He dropped his cigarette and crushed it out beneath his shoe. "You remember the book *Hotel?*"

"I remember the picture," Reardon said, and wondered what Wilkins was driving at.

"Same thing. I saw the picture, too, and they made the same mistake. Remember where the Countess, or whatever she was, said she was driving the hit-run car instead of her husband, the Earl, or the Duke, or something? Where it made such a big difference who was driving, and they hired the hotel dick to drive the car away, or something? Well, nobody even bothered to check the position of the front seat when it was down in the garage, after they drove it in after the hit-run. Not even the hotel dick! Sure, maybe the dame would have remembered to change the seat to the proper placement for her size, together with the rear-view mirror, the side-view mirror, the length of the seat-belt straps, and all, but I doubt it like hell. Anyway, in the book, and the movie, too, they didn't even check. Well, we do. We check out little things like that." He shrugged and smiled faintly. "Books—movies!"

It was a long speech for Lieutenant Wilkins, and he might even have amplified on the things his department had the sense to do

74

that books and movies overlooked, if the sound of rapidly approaching footsteps hadn't interrupted him. The two men looked down the dim aisle between the rows of parked cars to see Captain Clark approaching. The Accident Prevention Bureau reported to Traffic, not that they wouldn't have greatly preferred being reponsible to any other department.

"Reardon," Clark said briefly, his cold eyes passing over the Homicide lieutenant without interest. "Wilkins." He gestured toward the car. "What do you have so far?"

"I'll have a report on your desk in an hour or so, Captain."

"That doesn't answer my question," Clark said coldly. "What I meant was, have you found anything immediately useful?"

Wilkins would have liked to ask if the captain meant did the men leave calling cards tucked under the sun visor, or a map with an arrow indicating their hideout, but it wouldn't have been advisable. Captain Clark had a short sense of humor and a long memory.

"No, sir."

"Well, keep after it, but don't take all day." Clark turned to consider Reardon. "How about that what's-his-name upstairs? Did you get a chance to talk to him yet? The wop?"

"His name is Lazaretti. He's Italian," Reardon said. He was sure that Clark would have used the word "wop" if he had been addressing his question to Dondero. One day, possibly, Clark would pull a line like that with Captain Giordano of the Loft Squad and get his thick head handed to him. With Lieutenant Reardon's lousy luck, though, he wouldn't be there to see it. On the other hand, maybe he'd make captain himself, one day, and take on the job of cutting Clark down to size himself. Or maybe someday he wouldn't wait until he made captain. "Dondero's talking to the man now," he said, and thought that one way or the other Don ought to be finished with the little man by now.

"Yeah," Clark said unenthusiastically, almost as if it were his own instructions being carried out, and not too well, either. "Wilkins, I'll be waiting for your report. Soon. Don't take all day with it, hear? I've got plenty of other work for you."

"Yes, sir," Wilkins said, and watched the stumpy figure march away toward the elevator. "Someday . . . !" he said under his breath, and then looked at Reardon, smiling ruefully. "How it goes!"

"I know what you mean," Reardon said, smiling back, and followed Clark toward the elevator, although with every intention of waiting for the following car before going up to his office.

Saturday—3:20 P.M.

Lieutenant Reardon came into his office to find Dondero slumped dispiritedly in a chair, staring down at his folded hands, his rugged face expressionless. The lieutenant dropped into his chair and waited. When Dondero made no attempt to look up, Reardon picked up the telephone book from the corner of his desk, held it out at arm level, and let it drop. Dondero's head came up at the noise.

"Well," Reardon said with satisfaction, "it's alive, at least." He bent to retrieve the phone book, replaced it, and leaned back. "All right, what did our friend Lazaretti have to say?"

"Not much," Dondero said, and shook his head. There was a touch of admiration in his tone. "You wouldn't think a guy the size of a Crackerjack prize would have that much moxie, would you? He's a tough little monkey."

"Nothing at all?"

"Oh, his cousin in Brooklyn's name is Anthony Lazaretti, and I just got through talking to him and he's got a small fruit store and the last time he saw Guillermo was when they were kids, and he swears he didn't know his cousin was in the States, and for what it's worth, I believe him. If we have to, we can have the New York cops check him out, but I don't think it's necessary. And our friend also admits that Patrone isn't quite as much a stranger to him as he made out before, but other than those two bits of jeweled knowledge, we're where we were before. What he's doing here, what Patrone is doing here, what this whole case is all about —those things still rank as mysteries."

"What were the two fighting about?"

Dondero shrugged. "The one thing I'm sure of is that the fight was not part of any plan. Whatever the two are doing here, spending time in our jail wasn't part of the original program. They were probably fighting about the same important things most people fight about. Nothing."

"And you're sure he wasn't here in San Francisco for the reason he gave—just for a visit?"

Dondero sighed. "Anything's possible. Maybe years ago he pulled a thorn out of some guy's paw in the Colosseum, and when the guy heard he was in jail here in San Francisco, he kidnapped Pop to spring him in gratitude. Who knows? He may really have come here for a visit. The only thing is, I give twelve to one against, and those are better odds than I give against today being Thursday."

"Did you mention Pop Holland's name to him?"

"That I did, in a roundabout way. It rang no bell. I give eleven to six the little man never heard of Pop Holland in his life."

"Did you get a chance to talk to the other guy? The one Lazaretti was fighting with? Patrone?"

Dondero smiled. "No. I'm saving him for when we get stuck."

Reardon was not amused. "Did you check their passports?"

"Yeah. Like Zelinski so accurately reported—for him—both passports are fairly old, both men have legal visas, and this is the first time in the life of these passports either one of them was used for entrance into the United States."

"They came together?"

"That's one of the big confessions I got, which doesn't seem much in exchange for a skinned knuckle." He glanced down at the knuckle. "Just don't ask me why they came here, together or alone."

Reardon got up and began pacing up and down the office, or as much as he could in the limited space provided for junior officers at the Hall of Justice. He paused and looked down at Dondero.

"If Lazaretti or Patrone didn't know anyone here in town, maybe the guy who snatched Pop knew them in Italy?"

"Maybe," Dondero said. The idea didn't thrill him. "You want me to go to Rome and start checking? I speak fair Italian."

"Did you call the Italian Consulate yet? Or Interpol?"

"That comes next. Momma's only got two hands. But I don't expect he's got any big record or he wouldn't have gotten a passport. Or a visa." Dondero frowned. He looked up. "Jim, why are we complicating a simple problem? Why the hell don't we simply kick this Lazaretti character down the front steps and go home and get some rest? Or why don't we gift-wrap the son-of-a-bitch and deliver him where and when the man wants? And get Pop back and *then* go home and get some rest?"

"Ask Chief Boynton," Reardon said wearily. "He's got a lot of reasons that sounded good at the time, but don't ask me what they were." He yawned and stretched. "God, I'm tired! Well, you call the Italian Consulate, and get off some wires to Interpol, and let me see if I can get some work done."

He stared at the pile of papers in his in-basket, and shook his head disconsolately. The kidnapping of a police officer, like the murder of a police officer, ranked number one on any Hall of Justice priority list, but unfortunately that did not wipe out the hundreds of other cases that dragged themselves across the police blotter daily. He pulled the basket closer, picked up the top report to struggle through, and then became aware that Dondero was addressing him.

"I don't know about you," Dondero was saying, his finger holding his place in the telephone book, "but I didn't have any lunch and it's after four. Why don't we give it the old college try for another hour or so and then knock off and go down to the Wharf for a couple beers and a decent meal for a change?"

Reardon smiled. "Sorry, I've got a date." He saw the surprised look on Dondero's face and added, "It's with Jan. I forgot to tell you; we're back together again."

"Oh!" Dondero raised his eyebrows. He picked up the telephone and started to dial. "That explains a lot of things."

"Such as?"

"Such as the yawning," Dondero said, and grinned. "And also why you haven't solved this case yet. You never could keep your mind on two things at the same time."

CHAPTER 7

Sunday—3:00 A.M.

Reardon was having a dream. Under a completely neutral sky that almost looked like a drop cloth rather than a real sky, he drove quickly and confidently down a deserted road that twisted and turned between endless darkened warehouses. Though his neutral sky exhibited neither moon nor stars, and there were no streetlights nor headlamps to his car, somehow there seemed to be ample illumination, and though he did not know where he was going, he was sure he would recognize the place when he got there.

Ahead and slightly below there was a sudden bright cluster of lights, and he slowed the vehicle he was piloting—for now it was a tiny airplane—bringing it carefully through the tangle of overhead wires with skillful slips and edgings and stops and starts, to set the craft gently down alongside the roadway beside a narrow bridge. Then, without consciously alighting from the plane, he found himself with a noisy group at the top of a well-lit flight of stairs that led downward beside the small bridge to the water below. It reminded him of Paris, as seen in the movies, which was the only way he had ever seen Paris, with the Seine twisting through the city and these sets of steps at every bridge leading to the quays below, and suddenly he was in a gay mood, ready for celebration. Among the group with him he recognized Dondero and Captain

79

Tower and Frank Wilkins, although Captain Clark was missing, and he found himself pleased at this. A band was playing from below and he found himself anxious to get down the steps and join the festivities.

He handed over flying goggles and a leather jacket to the waiter from Marty's who had advised him of the telephone call the night before, and then he was hurrying down the steps to join the others, who presumably had preceded him, but when he reached the bottom he found he had somehow managed to get himself on the opposite side of the narrow channel, and that the music and the tables and Dondero and Tower and the rest were across the water from him, sitting near the band with drinks in their hands and obviously enjoying themselves.

At first he thought it was merely a joke, his having been put across the river from the party; all he had to do was to climb the steps, cross the bridge, and descend on the proper side to join the others, but when he looked up he saw that the steps weren't the wide stone steps he had descended but were the narrow grating type used on fire escapes, and that they twisted and turned to disappear into infinite blackness, and he knew if he started up them, when he came down the other side, if he could ever find the other side, the restaurant would be gone.

For a moment he wondered if possibly he might be dreaming, one of those endlessly frustrating uncomfortable dreams from which one had to awaken to escape the overwhelming tension; but then he saw there was a small rowboat tied to the jetty on his side of the water, and he knew he was not in any dreaded impossible position, because all he had to do was row across and he would be with the others.

He climbed into the rowboat, pleased to see that it was dry and equipped with oars, and set out, facing the other shore and pushing on the oars as his father had taught him when he wanted to see where he was rowing. But the harder he pushed, the farther away the other side of the narrow stream appeared, and the larger the boat in which he was riding, until he found himself at the prow of a large liner steaming silently through the night. He stared helplessly out into the darkness, searching for the shoreline and the lights, and thought desperately, *I'll have to warn them somehow that I won't be able to get to the party.* Then Mike Holland was at his side, dressed in his police uniform, and he knew that Mike was one of the officers on the ship. And Mike said comfortingly, *I'll warn them with the ship's whistle.* But instead of the deep throaty rumble of the ship's whistle, what came out of the whistle was the high soprano shrilling of a bell, and it rang and it rang and he wanted Mike to stop it, but it kept on ringing. . . .

Reardon rolled over, annoyed at the racket, coming from his dream slowly and with effort. The ringing would not go away, and he tried to sit up, hampered a bit in his efforts by Jan's arm across his chest. He lifted it tenderly and placed it to one side, groping in the dark for the telephone. He raised the receiver, still trying to bring himself back from the compelling grip of the dream, from the unknown but frightful dread he had felt on the liner's deserted deck to the warm security of the darkened bedroom.

"Hello? Yes?"

"Lieutenant Reardon?"

Sleep tried to escape but was checked by the remnants of the dream. Reardon squeezed his eyes tightly shut and then opened them wide, fighting the anesthesia of his almost coma-like sleep. The voice sounded faintly familiar. Probably one of the new men in Communications, Reardon thought sleepily, and yawned deeply, hoping the call was nothing that might drag him from his warm bed, although his subconscious was happy it had brought him from that ghastly liner and that invisible shoreline. Somehow he felt he had been saved from a terrible experience by being wakened. The voice in his ear repeated itself, a bit sharper in tone.

"Lieutenant Reardon!"

"Yeah, this is Reardon. . . ."

"Good. Did I wake you?"

Sleep fled and this time kept its distance. It was a voice Reardon had sworn he would never forget for the rest of his life, and he kicked himself for not having recognized it immediately. He reached up and flicked on the lamp over the bed, glancing at the clock on the nightstand, automatically registering the hour in his mind.

"What do you want?"

There was a dry, humorless chuckle.

"So you're finally awake and know who you're speaking to. Good!"

"What do you want?"

"What do I want? That's rather a stupid statement, you know? I told you before what I want. I want Guillermo Lazaretti! I thought I had made that abundantly clear in my tape, but apparently you people thought I was not serious. Well, believe me, I was! If you—"

"How's Mike Holland?"

The voice continued as if there had been no interruption. It almost sounded like a tape, with the lack of personal inflection. Reardon strained to hear, but the mechanical bumping sound that had been present in the tape was now lacking.

"—search the small ledge under the bridge that crosses the Islais Creek Channel, along the south side of the channel, I think you'll discover something that may convince you I'm really quite serious. Now, listen to me and listen carefully! I expect you people to stop your foolishness and drop Guillermo Lazaretti off at the bridge at two tomorrow morning. My patience, my friend, is not unlimited. If you search the ledge beneath the bridge you'll know I mean what I say. The instructions for delivering Lazaretti remain the same. Follow them!"

The telephone was hung up abruptly. Reardon instantly clicked the button until he got a dial tone and then quickly dialed. The telephone at the other end rang once and was answered.

"Police Department. Sergeant Silvestre."

Reardon was pleased that Silvestre was on duty; at least he knew his orders would be carried out quickly and efficiently. He swung his feet over the side of the bed, leaning over the receiver, blanking his mind to what might be found under the bridge.

"Sergeant—this is Lieutenant Reardon. First, I want to put a tracer on a call that was made to my home number just a minute ago. The call came in at 3:04 exactly. Once you've put the tracer in motion, call me back."

"Right," Silvestre said, and hung up.

Reardon hung up and slid from bed, padding quietly to the chair in one corner, where his clothes were draped. He dragged on his trousers, pulled his turtleneck over his head, and sat down to put on his shoes and socks. He came to his feet, trying to scrape his hair into some semblance of order with his fingers. Jan was watching him quietly from the bed. "Emergency," he said, and tried to make the word sound innocuous.

Jan glanced at the clock and then looked at him. "You haven't had much sleep."

He smiled. "It's getting to be the story of my life. A policeman's lot . . ." He felt it was better for him to say it, than for her; although since Jan had come back there had been surprisingly little talk about the problems of his job. "I'll try to catch a nap this afternoon."

Jan sat up. "Time for coffee?"

"I'll get some down at the Hall. You go back to sleep." The phone rang and he walked back to the bed to pick it up. "Yes?"

"Sergeant Silvestre, sir. We've put the tracer in motion."

"Good. Sergeant, which patrol car is nearest Third and Army?"

"Just a second, sir." Reardon waited, picturing Silvestre and the large electronics locations map on the Communications Center wall. "Potrero Five, sir. It's at General Hospital."

"In service or out?"

"Just came back in. They delivered a stab victim to emergency; no ambulance available."

"All right," Reardon said. "Tell them to get over to Third Street. There's a small bridge that crosses Islais Creek Channel just a couple of blocks south of Army. Tell them to get under the bridge, on the south side. There's a ledge there, and there's supposed to be a package on the ledge. I want it."

Silvestre, at his end, frowned.

"Do you have any idea what's in the package, sir? I mean, is it a job for the bomb squad, maybe?"

"No, it isn't a bomb—"

Reardon paused, frowning. Could it be a bomb? Was that what the unknown man meant to use to convince the police he was serious? It was highly doubtful, but why take a chance? Also, what the hell! Let the Bomb Squad be dragged out of bed like everybody else.

"You may be right," he said. "Send Potrero Five plus the

squad. Whatever they find, assuming it isn't a bomb, have them bring to the Hall. I'll be there when they get there." In one way, he thought, it would be far better if it were a bomb, rather than what I'm afraid it might be.

"Yes, sir. Anything else?"

Reardon thought a moment. The kidnapper had definitely sounded sincere, as if he meant business. And, if he had to be wakened, as well as the members of the Bomb Squad, why not make it a full house?

"Sergeant, can you arrange to tie me into a conference call? To both Chief Boynton and Captain Tower?"

"At this hour? You mean, wake them, sir?"

"That's what I mean."

"Oh, sure I can do it, sir. Just hang on."

Reardon waited, wondering if the small bridge bore any resemblance to the bridge he had pictured in his dream, and then put the thought away as voices began to mix on the line.

Sunday—4:15 A.M.

Four men sat around Chief Boynton's office on the fourth floor of the Hall of Justice: Chief Boynton, Captain Tower, Lieutenant Reardon, and Roy Gentry, head of Laboratory Services. Of the four only the chief appeared to be rested, as if he had had a full night's sleep, which he obviously had not. The window had been opened to allow some of the cigarette and pipe smoke to escape, and also to avoid the imagined odor that might have emanated from the covered laboratory dish that lay in the middle of the table. Fortunately, the laboratory dish that Gentry had selected was made of frosted Pyrex, so the contents were a mere shadow against the milky walls, but every man in the room could visualize with repugnance the contents of the dish.

From beyond the open window came night noises: the distant hooting of a deep-throated whistle from the bay, the high whine of tires on the pavement below, a sudden burst of laughter from some late revelers passing on Bryant. Inside the room the four men steadily contemplated the laboratory dish, each one with his own thoughts. For inside the closed frosted Pyrex dish lay a human finger, now separated from the wedding ring that had adorned it when the laboratory had first received the bloody specimen for examination.

Gentry crushed out his cigarette and immediately lit another. He took a deep drag, shoved his glasses up farther on his large bony nose, and spewed smoke as he spoke.

"It's Mike Holland's finger, all right. Print checks. The ring—"

He reached into his pocket and brought it out, sliding it across the desk. It came to rest a few inches from the small dish; nobody reached out to pick it up.

"—it's Mike's. Initials and dates. From a double-ring ceremony, I guess."

Boynton grunted. He, as well as the others, had never really doubted the fact since the gruesome package had been recovered and delivered to the Hall. He frowned at Gentry.

"Was it cut from a living man or a dead one?"

"We thought of that," Gentry said, and pushed his glasses up again. "Dr. Lascowski was down in the morgue on night duty, and I showed it to him. We agreed. We don't know."

Reardon had been staring at the little dish without really seeing it. Instead he saw a man being held down while someone else, some faceless person, chopped off one of his fingers. He spoke without raising his eyes from the dish.

"Pop's alive."

Boynton swung around to stare at him. "What makes you so sure, Lieutenant?"

"They need him alive, if they have to cut off any more fingers," Reardon said, and raised his eyes from the dish to look at the chief. "Or they think they do."

Boynton took Reardon's stare for a moment and then went back to Gentry, changing the subject.

"Did the amputation indicate any degree of medical knowledge? Was it done by a doctor, for example?"

Gentry shrugged. "We discussed that, Lascowski and me. It doesn't take any surgical skill to cut off a finger. If you put the finger over the edge of a table, or a wood chopping block, with the other fingers down alongside the edge of the table"—he demonstrated with one hand against the edge of the desk—"then all you need do is take a sharp knife or a hatchet—"

"Understood," Boynton said abruptly, cutting off the detailed description. He looked at each man in turn, and then sighed. "I know what you're thinking," he said heavily. "Still, the situation really hasn't changed. Our reasons for not acceding to this man's demands remain exactly the same, as far as I can see." He looked around the room again, and then shrugged. "However, since it's obvious you don't all agree with me, or you think we should make the exchange whether you agree with me or not—"

Reardon's hope's rose. By God, the chief was going to do it!

"—I'll take the matter up with the Board of Commissioners this morning as soon as I can get them together. I'll abide by their decision. But that's as far as I can go."

Reardon's hopes plummeted. The Board of Commissioners weren't cops; they couldn't possibly understand the feelings of the men on the force toward a fellow officer in a jam. Still, they were reasonable people, all with families; they ought to be able to put themselves in Pop's position. And, after all, letting Lazaretti go wouldn't be putting some hardened criminal on the street. The man hadn't committed any great crime, and besides, he would have been on an airplane for Rome, extradited, a few hours after he was released, in any event. So, possibly, if Boynton presented the case to the board in the proper perspective . . . But, the question was, would Boynton?

The chief might have been reading Reardon's mind.

"The senior department heads will be present and allowed to give their opinions to the board, as well," he said dryly, and looked around. "Well, anything else before we break up?"

"What about that tape?" Reardon asked.

Gentry spoke up, reaching for a cigarette and his lighter as he did so.

"First, as to that background noise—that bumping sound. We haven't been able to identify it. Now, as to the voice and identification of the speaker, we did a little better there. We graphed the voice and fed it into the comparitor. You gentlemen realize, I'm sure, that these voice machines are far from definitive; they only compare with other data prerecorded and fed the computer. You also realize they aren't too accurate."

"We know," Chief Boynton said in a tone that urged Gentry to get down to facts.

"Yes, sir. Well, among ourselves we break the possibilities into three areas: a presumptive level, which we consider fairly high; a conjecture level, which is a lower probability of accuracy, and"—Gentry smiled, a brief, humorless smile, quite professorial—"a pure guess level, I guess you could call it."

"Gentry—"

"Yes, sir," Gentry said, and hurried on, even foregoing lighting his cigarette. "Well, in regard to this particular tape, Ruth Damrosch ran the tests, and as you know she's the best technician we have. She's had the most experience—"

"Gentry!"

"Yes, sir," Gentry said, and finally got down to cases. "The man, according to our presumptions, has lived in the bay area for most of his life, or at least long enough in his formative years to establish his basic speech pattern and tonal definition. There also seems to be a total lack of probability of any Italian in his background, by which I mean any influence from parents, grandparents, or neighborhood environmental forces. In fact, we would judge his background to be British, most probably with a good degree of Scottish in his ancestry."

He stopped. Boynton frowned.

"That's all?"

"That's all, sir."

"What about the tape itself?"

"The cassette? There were no prints, as you know. The tape was a Memorex 60, available in about every department store, radio shack, tape house, anywhere. These cassettes have no serial number or factory identification of any kind."

Chief Boynton fell silent. Reardon spoke up.

"You said you hadn't been able to identify that funny bumping noise. Are you still trying?"

"We'll try again today, but we don't have much hope we'll find anything." He finally managed to light his cigarette and puffed on it in relief. "You see," he said, "we don't have a large library of sounds for comparative purposes, and if we did, I doubt it would be very useful. Most of the standard sound records are made up of sounds we would all recognize without the help of any machine—birds, railroad sounds, automobile racing sounds, animal sounds, car crashes, baby sounds, that sort of thing; libraries primarily built up to be used on soundtracks of films, or TV tapes. Ruth separated that background sound from the voice and fed it into our comparator against the few sounds we have, and"—again there was the brief, classroom-type smile—"all it did was shake its head."

The silence that fell now was unbroken. Boynton came to his feet.

"What you're saying," he said, "is that the man could be almost anyone in this area—with the possible exception of the Italians living here—and the sound in the background could be anything at all. Great."

Gentry looked down. "I'm sorry. . . ."

"Nobody's blaming you. It's just that we're not getting anywhere on this damned case, and it's beginning to get under my skin." He looked at his watch. "Well, gentlemen, I think that's enough for tonight. I'm going home and try to get a few hours rest. I suggest you all do the same."

He nodded abruptly, looked around the room to see if anyone felt like disagreeing with him, and then marched through the door. Gentry started to follow and then remembered his exhibits. He reached across the desk, retrieved them, and muttered a hurried good-bye as he trotted from the room. Captain Tower had been silent throughout the meeting; now he came to his feet, stretched, and looked at Reardon.

"Better go home and get some sleep, Jim."

Reardon yawned. "I'll catch a couple hours in the gym," he said, "as soon as I check Communications." He drew the telephone closer and pressed the button. Silvestre answered.

"Communications, Sergeant Silvestre."

"Silvestre, this is Lieutenant Reardon. What about that tracer?"

"No dice, sir. With the new equipment the phone company's installing, about the only way you can trace a call these days is by having a bug on the line."

"Great!" Reardon muttered, and hung up. "The phone company's getting too damn mechanical for its own good," he said half to himself, and remembered something else. He looked up. "Captain, about that board meeting tomorrow—"

"I know," Tower said quietly. "I know. And so do the rest of the department heads. Don't worry, Jim. We'll speak our piece."

CHAPTER 8

Sunday—12:10 P.M.

The night was a huge black box with no bottom, top, nor sides, and Reardon was surprised that he was no longer frightened to be back aboard the mysterious liner. He looked around for Mike Holland, but the deck was deserted. Beneath his feet he could feel the steady pulsing of the ship's engines. There was something faintly familiar about the even, rhythmic bumping, like a background soundtrack to something he was acquainted with; but he did not dwell on the thought. Far more important exploration lay before him. This was a new life, totally separated from the small bridge over the narrow channel, and the party and the band and his friends there. This was adventure!

He turned from a view of the endless ocean, stretching to the same neutral sky hung like a drape in the background, and found himself looking with pleased excitement into the depths of the ship's hold, and was surprised and pleased at hearing voices and seeing men and knowing he was not alone on the ship. He leaned over the hatch coaming, peering down. On the deck far below, wreathed in vapors and spotlighted with huge klieg lights, barebacked sweating figures were working swiftly over a large form hidden in the steam and the shadows, and Reardon suddenly realized he was on a whaler, watching the long sharp pole knives stabbing away, expertly slicing the wide strips of blubber from the inert shape.

He suddenly wanted to be with the others, all those fine men, friends, fellow crewmen, brother whalers!—and then he was down in the hold, bare-chested, sweating in the steam, reaching out eagerly like the others with his long pole knife at the shapeless form on the floor, but then he saw with shock that it was Mike Holland spread-eagled there, and the men were jabbing at his out-stretched hand while Mike tried to avoid them by turning and twisting his wrist. Reardon found himself struggling to get through the crowd of men to reach Mike's side, but the harder he fought, the farther back in the crowd he found himself, until he wasn't in the ship at all but in a subway train, one of the Bart cars, plunging through a black tunnel, full of people, and he was trying to break his way through to the car ahead, where he knew he'd find Mike, and then just as he managed to get the door be-tween the cars open, he saw that there were no cars ahead, just the endless tunnel, and there on the tracks he thought he saw a man up ahead, tied across the rails, and he could see, as if with zoom vision, one hand spread on the rail the same way Gentry had demonstrated, one finger along the edge, the others at right angles, and he turned to the motorman to make him stop the car, but hands pulled him back from the small door until he tore him-self loose with a final wrench and was rolling across a varnished floor, bumping his elbow painfully.

"Man!" Lundahl said admiringly. "When you sleep, you really sleep, don't you, Lieutenant!"

"Ghaaa!" Reardon sat up groggily, rubbing his elbow, aware of the bare floor beneath him and the pile of gym mats he had been sleeping on, off to one side. If I keep up like this, he thought sourly, I'm going to have to sleep in a crib, with railings all around. He yawned deeply and shook his head violently, trying to work off the horror of the dream enough to enable him to look at Lundahl with a modicum of intelligence.

"What time is it?"

Lundahl checked his watch, then verified it with the big gym clock on one wall. "A little after noon."

Reardon sat more erect. "What!" He looked around. "Where the hell was that recruit class that works out here at eight o'clock? I figured they'd wake me."

"It's Sunday, Lieutenant," Lundahl aaid gently. "September fifth." He smiled faintly. "I'm scared to tell you the year, because you'll accuse me of swiping your beard and your bowling ball and maybe even your little dog. . . ."

Reardon grunted, unamused, and came to his feet stiffly. He rubbed his face, trying to bring some life to the rubbery, inert skin, and then looked around the deserted gymnasium while he stretched. If there was anything in the world more deserted-looking than a gymnasium with only the smell of old socks for company, he couldn't imagine what it was. He put the pointless thought away and tried to bring his mind back to business.

"What about the board meeting on Mike Holland?"

"They're still at it, hot and heavy," Lundahl said. "They've been at it since a little after nine this morning. They just sent out for some sandwiches, so maybe Mike has a chance, at that."

"Let's hope." Reardon yawned. He still felt groggy, still felt the edge of his dream. What he needed was a hot cup of coffee, or a cold glass of beer, or both. He started to dust himself off, and then paused, frowning. "So if nothing's new, why the rush to wake me up?" Not, he had to admit, that he was unhappy to be rid of his dream; he was sure he didn't want to be riding on that subway car when it ran over that hand!

"Oh, yeah," Lundahl said, suddenly remembering. "I didn't want to wake you up at all, at first, not just for some nut call, but then I figured, what the hell, if it happened to be important, which I'm sure it isn't, then I'm in the doghouse for not telling you."

"Whenever you get through with the self-analysis . . ."

"Yeah. Like I said, it was a nut call for you. Some character calls up on the phone and wants to tell you he was Mo House, the First."

Reardon stared. "What?"

"That's it, Lieutenant. Like I said, a nut. He even spelled it. M. O. House, the First. He wanted us to pass it on to you as soon as possible. And that was the entire message." He frowned as a sudden thought struck him. "Hey! That M.O.—could that be, like, modus operandi?"

Reardon suddenly laughed. Mo House, the First, eh? The message was clear enough, now; Porky Frank wanted to meet him at Marty's Oyster House at one o'clock. The wild code he and Porky employed from time to time may have had something to do with security at one time, but that time had long passed. Now the code was reinvented constantly, used as a form of one-upmanship on the part of the two, and Reardon had to give Porky credit for brevity with this one, if nothing else.

Lundahl was watching him closely. "It didn't mean modus operandi, huh, Lieutenant? And it wasn't a nut call, either, was it?"

"Just a code," Reardon said, coming back to life from his nap. "It was my broker telling me that Mohouses are going up on the first." He glanced over his shoulder and dropped his voice. "Don't blab it all over the place. We don't want it to get around."

Lundahl looked hurt. "You mean, if you wanted me to know what it was all about, you'd tell me, right?"

"Right," Reardon said, pleased with Lundahl's ready intelligence, and led the way from the gymnasium, not unhappy to leave his dream behind in the large vaulted room, keeping company with the dust and the odor of stale socks.

Sunday—1:05 P.M.

Marty's Oyster House, in common with most bars and restaurants in that section of San Francisco, was far from being overly busy on an early Sunday afternoon, but that in no way tended to improve its notoriously terrible service. Porky Frank, sitting in a booth to the rear, saw Reardon begin to push through the etched-glass doors and put out a hand, catching a waiter on the wing. Porky's surprise was even greater than that of his bagged quarry; the waiters at Marty's were usually more elusive. Still, Porky had one and he did not intend to free him until he had put him to good use.

"An extra dry martini, up, and a large beer," he said, disregard-

93

ing the hurt look on the face of the waiter. "The martini with a olive."

The waiter nodded, unsurprised at the order. Anyone impolite enough to snatch at waiters instead of letting them come to you at their own pace was quite apt to be the type to use a beer chaser for a martini. Still, one of the rules of the house was that once you were pressed into service whether against your will or not, you actually had to serve the customer. It was a rule the waiters at Marty's intended to fight bitterly at their next contract negotiations, but for the moment it was in effect.

"Dry olive and beer," he said into his drooping mustache, and headed for the bar.

Reardon dropped into the booth across from Porky and nodded. Porky returned the greeting and considered the lieutenant gravely for a moment before coming to the conclusion that enough preliminaries had been observed and that it was time to move on.

"You look rested, Mr. R," he said equably. "Tell me, what's new on the case?"

Reardon looked around for a waiter and saw with astonishment that one was approaching their table laden with martini and beer, and seemed intent upon serving them. He turned back to Porky with a frown of curiosity.

"It was nothing," Porky said modestly. "I caught him when he wasn't looking."

"But you caught him, which is what counts." Reardon's tone was properly congratulatory. He looked around and realized he was hungry. He accepted his beer, held the waiter by the arm while he ordered a hot roast beef sandwich with mashed potatoes. The waiter shrugged philosophically, and wrote it on his pad. What people did with their stomachs was no concern of his. Reardon released the waiter and turned to Porky. "Well?"

"I asked you first," Porky said a bit reprovingly. He saw the look that crossed Reardon's face but was not intimidated. "I repeat, I asked you first. Mainly because there is nothing new from my end. I wanted to meet with you to see if you had anything. Maybe it would tie in with the nothing I've got. You understand?"

"Roughly." Reardon took a large draught of his beer and set

the glass down. He wiped his lips and considered Porky. "We received the tape, the way the man said on the telephone. Somebody had bumped into a mailman and slipped the package into the mailbag while he was helping the mailman pick up the junk. You were right on that. . . ."

Porky looked modest.

"We even found the wino who'd put the package in the mailbag," Reardon added. "Only he was dead. . . ."

Porky's look of modesty disappeared. Reardon related the events of the past few days while Porky listened closely, taking a sip every now and then of his martini. The waiter brought the food, placed it on the table with an air of refusing any responsibility for it, and escaped before these exigent customers could demand anything else, like water, or toothpicks, or even dessert. Reardon took a mouthful, found it delicious, and spoke around it.

"And that's where we are," he said. "Nowhere. This bastard is cutting Pop into little squares and the brains are trying to make up their minds whether to trade this Lazaretti for him or not." He dug another large forkful of food from his plate and sighed. "Not that I'm so damned sure the brains are wrong. It's just that it makes it a little rough on Pop." He put the food in his mouth, chewed, swallowed, and looked at Porky somberly. "And you say there's nothing from your end? Does anything I just told you tie into anything you've heard? In any way?"

Porky shook his head. "Not that I can see."

"Anything about any Italian connection?"

Porky's eyebrows rose. "Italian?"

Reardon finished the last bit, looked at the plate as if he might well have liked to lick it, and put down his fork regretfully. He picked up his beer.

"That's right. Italian. Lazaretti is from Italy, and Lazaretti is the guy this maniac wants to trade for Pop. And we can't figure out why."

"Nor can I."

"Great," Reardon said with irritation. "You must have done some great listening!"

"Oh, I listened very well, and I heard quite a lot," Porky said easily. "It's just that I fail to see any connection with what I heard and what you would like to hear. For example, I hear there's apt to be a change in gambling bosses in town—not that the Organization exists, you understand, or if it exists it certainly has no tentacles planted in our fair city, and even if by some odd coincidence it did have a tentacle or two around, certainly nothing to do with gambling. Still, the rumor persists."

Reardon was listening. Porky went on.

"Then, too, I hear that the price of Turkish horse is on the rise, due to a temporary shortage, such as occurs from time to time. I also hear there's a lot of heat on a few parties because it seems a three-hundred-grand shipment of grass from Mexico turned out to be just that. Grass. Like on your front lawn. Although, from my experience, real grass in Mexico is rarer than Mary Jane. Theoretically, that should make it more valuable, shouldn't it?"

"Depends on the going market for Mexican lawns," Reardon suggested.

"Probably. Let's see—what else did I hear? Oh, yes! Speaking of Mary Jane, the real big talk around is that there's a chemist in Monterey who has been working on the development of an essence that smells just like grade-A pot. Now that I think about it," Porky said, "I wonder why nobody ever did that before?"

"Why, for heaven's sake?" Reardon asked, astonished.

"Come, come, Mr. R!" Porky said reprovingly. "You can't be as obtuse as all that! Can you imagine the frustration of all the dogs the Federal Bureau of Narcotics has trained to sniff out marijuana, when just about everything that comes through customs has the same smell?" He laughed. "Can you picture the scene at customs, say when four or five planes come in at the same time from our sister republic to the south, and those poor mutts start going absolutely berserk over everyone's luggage? It'll look like a dog-food ad."

"Very comical, I'm sure," Reardon said dryly. "But it doesn't get us anywhere."

"No," Porky admitted, and sobered up. "Still, it's all I can offer at the moment. You're sure that this Lazaretti, or Sergeant Holland, never raised dogs for the Narcotics Bureau? It would give us a tie-in." He seemed to accept Reardon's silence as denial. "Too bad. Well, I shall return to keeping my ear to the ground.

Pray it doesn't rain. The one thing I hate is moldy ear, as we call it. Incidentally," he added curiously, "what did you ever do about that newspaperman?"

"Who?"

"You remember—that columnist you read so assiduously. The one who does that 'View from the Top of the Mark' or something."

" 'View from Nob Hill,' " Reardon said. "What about it?"

Porky sighed disappointedly.

"Do you, or do you not, recall that at our last meeting I suggested to you to contact this scrivener, place hot needles under his fingernails, if necessary, and extract from him a statement as to whether or not he mentioned in his column that you were in charge of the dinner arrangements for Mike Holland's testimonial dinner? And also, if not, how anyone could have learned of this vital fact? I believe I even labeled this a clue, hoping that with that nomenclature it would remain indelibly printed upon your policeman's brain."

"I remember."

"Good. I should hope so. I even wrote it on a piece of paper and placed it in your pocket."

"I remember."

"And you followed it up, of course?"

"No, I didn't," Reardon said, and fished in the breast pocket of his jacket. He withdrew the paper, studied it a moment, and crumpled it, tossing it into an ashtray. "If we start to waste time checking out dumb things like that, we'll really be in trouble. For a starter, we'd have half the people in town to check out, and we've got a lot more important things to work on."

"Such as?" Porky asked softly.

"Such as lots of things," Reardon said shortly, and reached into his pocket for money.

"My treat," Porky said, and put out a restraining hand. He smiled. "It'll be on your eventual bill, don't worry—properly inflated, but that's the modern way."

"Bill for what?" Reardon said dourly. "For the information you've delivered so far?"

Porky sighed. "Patience, Mr. R, patience . . ."

"Yeah," Reardon said brusquely, and came to his feet. "Patience, while Pop Holland gets chopped into little pieces!"

Sunday—2:30 P.M.

Detective Stan Lundahl came out of the elevator at the lobby floor of the Hall of Justice, paused to light a cigarette, turned in the direction of the large front doors, and almost bumped into his superior.

"Hi, Lieutenant," Lundahl said, pleased to see a familiar face on a dull Sunday afternoon. "Any decent information from your pigeon?" He saw the startled look on Reardon's face and laughed. "Well, hell, Lieutenant—any guy named Mo, ten to one he's a pigeon, right?"

"Stan," Reardon said, relieved, "you'll be a detective, yet. By the way, where are you off to?"

"Home," Lundahl said. "You got something for me to do? Connected with the Holland case," he added hastily. "Otherwise I'm supposed to be off duty right now. I'm on the graveyard shift for the next week, starting tonight."

Reardon tried to think of anything he wanted Lundahl to do on the Pop Holland case, but couldn't. His brain felt fogged. Too much sleep, he thought, or too much good living in the form of an occasional meal. Or maybe it was just that the effects of gym-sock miasma took a long time to wear off. He looked into Lundahl's waiting face.

"No, I guess not. Where's Don?"

"Home, too, I guess," Lundahl said. He looked around for a place to get rid of his cigarette stub and decided the lobby floor was the closest. He dropped it, and stood on it, ostrich-style. "After the board meeting, Don stormed out of the joint breathing fire and swearing like only Don can swear. Half Italian, half Fisherman's Wharf. He—" He saw the startled look that crossed Reardon's face. "Hey, that's right. You didn't know, did you?"

"No. But it was bad news, huh?"

"Yeah," Lundahl said. His voice turned bitter. "Can't make exceptions just because a man is a retired police officer, you know. Got to treat everyone alike—although I'd bet they'd trade Boynton himself if it was the mayor's wife being held! Same old argument! No cop's going to be safe on the street, we let Lazaretti go. Start trading convicts for cops, pretty soon the old jail's empty, and then where we all going to work?" He made a face and said a nasty word.

"Yeah," Reardon said in sympathy. "Anything else new?"

"That's the scoop."

"Well, go home and get some rest."

"Sure," Lundahl said. "If my in-laws aren't over for the day." He turned and jammed his way through the glass doors to the street.

Reardon stared after the tall detective a moment and then turned back toward the elevators. He took one to the fourth floor, walked along the unusually silent corridor to his office, and dropped into the chair behind his desk, looking around. The place was deserted, the men either on assignment or on Sunday time-off. Reardon sighed and reached for the in-basket.

The report on top was from Laboratory Services; a quick glance proved it to be the report covering the tape, and contained little beyond what Gentry had told them in the early morning meeting. He put it aside and picked up the next one. This report was a compilation of station house replies to a request from Chief Boynton's office, and indicated that copies had been sent to all departments, including Homicide. Captain Tower had scrawled his initials in one corner and had directed it to Lieutenant Reardon. Reardon settled back to read, but the words kept going past him without pausing long enough to deposit much meaning. He forced himself to go back to the beginning.

It amounted to nothing, but then, he thought, if any of the reports had amounted to anything, the Hall would have been jumping with activity instead of everyone having taken time off, as if the Holland case—not to mention a hundred other cases—had all been solved and filed. The report confirmed that the footmen from the various stations had checked out every possible visible telephone booth in the city without locating a single witness to a man in a booth with a tape recorder. Which was what Reardon had expected, and he marveled at the amount of wasted time that could be devoted to a pointless search for nothing. Which would be the same case if he wasted his time chasing down that newspaperman, the way Porky Frank would like. He tossed the report aside and picked up the next one.

Like the others, this one had been addressed to the chief with copies to Homicide among others, and had again filtered down via Captain Tower. It was from Robbery, and Davidson's men had gone over the Holland house from top to bottom, had checked the garage and the driveway, had spoken to neighbors in all directions, storekeepers, and even the manager of a nearby movie theater. And, like the previous report, it said nothing.

He tossed it aside, looked at the rest of the papers in his in-basket, drummed his fingers restlessly on the desk for a few moments while making up his mind, and then reached for the telephone. He got an outside line and dialed; there was a brief wait and then Jan was on the line. She sounded hurried.

"Hello?"

"Hello, Jan?"

"Hello, darling." Reardon felt better at once, just hearing the warmth that entered her voice. "Where are you?"

"At the Hall. Look, sweet, there's absolutely nothing doing at the moment and I'm about ready to climb a wall. How would you like to do something? There's a twi-night doubleheader at Candlestick, or we could take in a movie, or rob a bank, or anything. How about it?"

"I can't, darling." Jan sounded truly sorry. "I've got tons of work. Jake dropped off the plans for the new shopping mall, and I have to have all my comments ready for submittal through Jake tomorrow. . . ."

Reardon felt worse than he had before. He hadn't realized how much he had been subconsciously looking forward to seeing Jan. He needed her to lift away some of his depression, some of his feeling of growing helplessness in the case of Michael Patrick Holland; some of the feeling of guilt, in fact, that here he was trying to make the momentous decision as to whether to take in a doubleheader or a movie, when Pop was tied up someplace, and undoubtedly in a bad way. Still, when you have one of the town's upcoming architects for your girl friend, you have to be prepared for moments when she has to work to maintain her upcomingness.

"Not a chance, honey?"

"I'm sorry, darling." Jan had an idea. "But, why don't you come over here and watch the game on television? Or come over and take a nap? But I really mean a nap. No chasing the virtuous lady around a table." He could hear the smile in her voice, but he knew she meant it. "I really have to get these notes done tonight."

"No, I don't think so," Reardon said. He tried to keep the hurt from his voice, but he didn't feel like playing second fiddle that afternoon, not to a bunch of blueprints he couldn't make head or tail of, while Jan could. It somehow belittled his manliness, and he felt down enough as it was. "Maybe I'll go to a movie."

"You do that, darling." It was apparent from her tone that Jan's mind was already back on her shopping mall, with her head full of stresses and strains and beams and elevations and a thousand other things she understood that he didn't.

"Yeah, I'll do that. Maybe we can have dinner tomorrow night."

"Fine," Jan said, and he could tell her mind was not on him.

"Yeah," he said hopelessly, and hung up. He knew he was being foolish to feel put down by a few pieces of paper with unintelligible markings on them, but that was the way he felt at the moment. You'd think when he was down in the dumps, once in a million years, that Jan could sacrifice one lousy afternoon from her damned blueprints for some stupid buildings, or shopping mall, or something . . . !

He suddenly grinned, knowing how idiotic he was being. He knew exactly what his reaction would be if Jan asked him to halt in the middle of an important investigation and go over and hold her hand just because some elevation, or some roof line, or sewer plan on a drawing wasn't exactly what she desired. He'd tell her he was sorry, but the job came first; and that was roughly what she was telling him. And she was right.

Feeling better, he came to his feet and headed for the elevators and freedom. Desk work was out, that afternoon. No sitting in that empty office looking at a bunch of meaningless reports. No, damn it, he *would* go to the movies! Maybe one of the bright cops up there on the screen would show him where he was slipping up —where they were all slipping up—in their search for Pop Holland and his kidnapper or kidnappers.

He walked from the Hall, descended the steps, crossed the sidewalk, and climbed into his Charger, which was parked as usual, illegally, in front of the Hall. It was not that Lieutenant Reardon always parked there illegally; it was only when some other officer didn't beat him to it. He was feeling better as he started the engine, making plans. After the movie, he'd go out and have a meal at a resturant where the waiters didn't give you ulcers, and then go back to his apartment and watch "Mannix," or "Kojak," or another one of those flawless demonstrations of proper police procedure, and if he couldn't tolerate the tube, he might even read a book, if he hadn't forgotten how. Sherlock Holmes, maybe.

Whistling a tuneless ditty, he put the car into gear and headed for the center of town, forcing any thought of Mike Holland into the recesses of his mind, at least for the moment.

Monday—6 A.M.

Lieutenant James Reardon, feeling refreshed for what seemed to him to be the first time, possibly since childhood, opened his eyes, blinked in friendly fashion at the narrow band of sunlight that had managed to squeeze under the edge of the drawn shade, and then sat up in bed, stretching luxuriously in comfort. He swung his feet over the edge, wincing a trifle as they struck the bare floor, and then padded into the kitchen to put up coffee, noting with satisfaction that he had beaten the set alarm clock by a full forty-five minutes.

The evening before had been somewhat of a qualified success. The movie antihero cop had been duly nastier than the bad guys, had used language that would have gotten his mouth washed out with soap in a G-rated film, had taken graft and kicked little

102

children, had sold narcotics to kindergarteners, and was in the process of winning the girl when Reardon had walked out of the theater, feeling that the producers were only trying to make him feel good by comparison.

A decent meal at one of his favorite Japanese restaurants, however, had taken a portion of the bad taste away, and when he got back to his apartment he found that Kojak was not at all like the movie policeman, but even helped old ladies to cross the street, protecting them from vicious gunfire with his own body, and even sucking a lollipop as he did so. Reassured, Reardon had taken a straight two ounces of whiskey, followed it by a glass of milk, and then gone to bed at eleven o'clock to sleep the sleep of the just. Now, wide awake, full of vim and vigor and with his depression far behind, he put coffee into a percolator, filled the bottom portion with the requisite water, assembled the gadget, put the entire contraption on the stove, and sat down to watch the pretty little bubbles, listen to the gentle burping of the unit, and cogitate, once again, on the case of Pop Holland.

It was quite apparent, in the light of day, and with a good night's rest behind him, that there was no reason to allow depression or lack of self-confidence to interfere with the proper handling of the case. Nor was there time for self-pity. There were hundreds of things that could and should be done, and he wondered at himself for getting into a frame of mind so negative as to prevent himself from handling the case as he would have any other.

That hint of Porky's about the newspaperman, for example. Of course it was a long shot, and maybe even useless, but it had to be better than sitting at his desk, commiserating with himself, and spending the county's funds flipping paper clips into a wastebasket. The first thing this morning he'd go down to the paper, find out the name of the author, and ask him how he had known Reardon was in charge of the arrangements for Pop's dinner. Sure, it was a dumb question, but if there weren't any smart ones to ask, dumb ones would have to serve.

And while he was at the paper, he'd also ask about any reporters who might have brought in the story of the fight between

Lazaretti and Patrone. He'd forgotten all about that. And, in fact, he'd have a talk with Patrone; that was another thing Dondero was supposed to do, but he'd been laying off all the jobs on Dondero with one excuse or another. This time he'd do the interviewing, and Don would just be the translator. And this time he wouldn't allow any distaste for manhandling stop him from getting information. Dondero was right; while he was being delicate, Pop was getting skinned.

And there was the matter of Interpol, and the Italian Consulate, another two jobs he had ducked off to Dondero when there was no reason he shouldn't handle them himself. And the matter of the stuff Property was holding of both Lazaretti and Patrone—their wallets and their passports. Those were things he ought to check out himself, not leave to others. And the hotel where the two had been staying, or the friends they had stayed with if they hadn't been at a hotel. Hell, there was lots of work that had to be done!

He paused. The telephone was ringing in the bedroom. He turned the flame down under the coffee and walked back into the bedroom. This time the telephone hadn't brought him from any horror dream; this time he'd been awake and ready for it. He picked up the telephone receiver, ready for anything.

"Yes?"

"Lieutenant? This is Lundahl."

"Good morning, Stan." Reardon tried not to sound too pleased with life; after all, Detective Lundahl had been on the graveyard shift and was winding up a long night. "How's it going?"

"Not good, Lieutenant."

"Anything I can do?"

Lundahl cleared his throat uncomfortably. He hated to disturb lieutenants that early in the morning, especially with bad news.

"Yeah, Lieutenant. You can come down to the morgue. I got a hunch Captain Tower and maybe even the chief will be down pretty soon. They're calling them now."

A cold chill wiped away Reardon's previous ebullience.

"What happened?"

"We just fished a stiff out of the bay—"

"*Pop?*"

"Not Pop," Lundahl said, and bit back a yawn. It had been a long miserable graveyard shift. "Another poor bastard."

Reardon felt ashamed of his relief. After all, life had probably been sweet to whoever the victim was, and his family would feel his loss as much as or more than they would feel Pop's.

"Murdered?"

"Yeah. He looks bad. Somebody must have tried to get some information out of him using matches, and a candle, too, it looks like, because there were tallow stains, and what all. And then, when they either got what they were looking for, or when they got tired of playing games with him, it looks like they held his face under water until he just quit living."

Reardon made a face. "Messy, huh?"

"Real messy."

"Any identification?" Something else Lundahl had said suddenly struck Reardon. "And what's this about Captain Tower and maybe Chief Boynton coming down at this hour? Just for some stranger fished out of the bay?"

"Well, that's just the point," Lundahl said wearily. "He ain't exactly a stranger. There're going to be a lot of questions asked, Lieutenant—a lot of questions! Because we just got through checking out the stiff's identification, and according to the card, he wasn't supposed to be getting himself drowned out in the bay. He was supposed to be upstairs under our protection. His name was Lazaretti."

CHAPTER 9

Monday—8:20 A.M.

There were other men in Chief Boynton's office, many of them, but from the charged atmosphere it was plain that Lieutenant Anton Zelinski, in charge of Detention, and Patrolman Charles Travers, the night guard of the main cell block, considered themselves practically alone. Reardon thought that Zelinski's jaw looked hard enough to strike fire off of with flint, and if Travers was at all intimidated by his superior's belligerent appearance he didn't show it.

"Goddamn it, Lieutenant!" Travers was saying with what he obviously considered justifiable resentment, "a guy comes walking in with a paper, what am I supposed to do?"

"You should use your head, goddamn it!"

"Jeez, thanks!"

"Jeez, thanks, yourself! How many times somebody comes up to you at one o'clock in the morning with a prisoner release?" Zelinski asked with withering scorn. "Fifteen?"

"So maybe it was the first time," Travers admitted without backing down one inch. "So there's got to be a first time for everything, don't they?" He raised a thick finger in the lieutenant's face. "You ain't saying it wasn't a proper release form, you notice? You ain't saying that."

"So did you even bother to see whose John Hancock was on the release?" Zelinski demanded. "Or was that too complicated for you?"

Travers looked at the ceiling in supplication, and then brought his hot blue eyes back to the lieutenant's angry red face.

"No, I didn't bother to send the signature down to the lab if that's what you mean. I saw it was signed, that's enough. I honestly don't know who signs releases; Charley Finley, for all I know. Anyways, lots of judges sign releases, and I don't know all their signatures. This one was just a big scrawl, anyways. You couldn't hardly read it, even."

"My God!" Zelinski struck his head with exaggerated dramatics. "And the fact that a guy hands you a release form with a signature you can't even read—that don't mean a thing to you?"

"Jeez, Lieutenant, I can't even read *your* signature!"

"Except you know damn well I don't sign release forms for prisoners!"

Travers almost wailed in frustration.

"Damn it, Lieutenant, you ain't being fair! A *cop*—a sergeant I *know* is a cop—comes to me with a proper release form like I've seen hundreds of times, saying this Lazaretti is being transferred from the Hall to Soledad, and this sergeant I *know* is a cop tells me he's been assigned to accompany the prisoner." He appealed to the faces around him. "What in hell am I supposed to do? Refuse to honor a release? Tell the sergeant to go to hell?" He turned back to Zelinski. "Call you up at one o'clock in the morning and get reamed out for bothering you for nothing? Jeez, Lieutenant, try to see it from my angle!"

"I'll see it from your angle! I'll—"

Boynton had had enough. If he had previously thought any useful information might come out of the confrontation, he was pretty well convinced by now that it wouldn't. He banged on the table, breaking up the tête-à-tête.

"We're not getting anywhere," he said heavily. "Let's take it over again from the top." He swiveled about, looking at Captain Tower stonily. "As I understand it, Captain, your Sergeant Dondero went up to the cell blocks last night with a falsified release form and took a prisoner from custody. A prisoner, incidentally, that the board had specifically decided was not to be released. And a few hours later that prisoner, with every evidence of having been extensively tortured, is found dead. And now your Sergeant Dondero can't be located. Is that the case?"

Tower clenched his jaw. "Yes, sir." He was unhappy and both looked and sounded it. It was the first time since he had taken over Homicide that anything like this had happened, and in his mind he promised all subordinates silently and grimly that it would be the last. "We've checked everywhere he might be, but so far we've been unable to locate him. We've put an all-points out on the man, and we have a watch being kept on his apartment as well as on most of his known hangouts, in case he shows." Tower hesitated a moment and then went on, although he knew he was courting trouble. "Sir, do we have to give this story to the papers?"

Boynton's expression turned to rock.

"What are you suggesting? A cover-up for a cop? Then we'd *really* be in the—"

"No, that isn't it—"

"Then what the devil is it?" Chief Boynton studied the head of Homicide blackly. "And are you also trying to tell me the newspapers haven't got the story yet?"

"They've got the story about the body being found," Tower said, "but as far as they know, it's an unknown. They don't have his identity so far, and they don't know he was a prisoner here. They also don't know about the torture inflicted on the body, nor that a police officer is involved. Maybe if we—"

Boynton exploded. "Damn it, don't give me any 'maybes'! Maybe if more of our men were properly motivated, things like this wouldn't happen! And there's going to be no cover-up for this Dondero, I assure you of that!"

"What I'm trying to say," Tower said stubbornly, "is that it seems to me we ought to sit on as much of the story as we can until we get our hands on Dondero and hear his side—"

Zelinski snorted. He was still irritated at having the security of his detention cells violated.

"His side! What side? Hell, he was up there yesterday during the day and he had Lazaretti in the 'conference room' and beat the living crap out of him there." He jerked a contemptuous thumb. "Reardon was with him. Ask him."

All eyes swung to the lieutenant.

"Don was just trying to get information from the man, to help locate Pop Holland," he said quietly. "He was told to go up there for that purpose. It wasn't his own idea."

"Was he also told to beat the guy?" Zelinski asked with exaggerated politeness. "I heard about that interrogation session; my man had to take Lazaretti back to his cell. But Dondero couldn't do a proper job on Lazaretti inside the Hall, so he sneaks the guy outside at night and gives him the works. What side of what story can he have? That he had the tough luck to have Lazaretti die on him?"

"You're crazy!" Reardon promised himself to take Zelinski on in the next interdepartmental boxing matches and he meant to hammer on that thick skull until some sense dribbled in through the cracks. "Dondero isn't that kind of a cop!"

"I know," Zelinski said with exaggerated sympathy. "I know. He's also not the kind of cop to fake a release form, either. He's just a good, clean, one hundred per cent All-American boy with a heart of purest gold." He tried to look apologetic. "I'd stand at attention in his honor, only my feet hurt."

"You make a great judge-and-jury combination," Reardon said angrily. "I'm surprised Dondero didn't leave a full confession along with that fake release form; then we could put out a shoot-on-sight order and get it over with!"

Boynton's fist bounced off his desk blotter.

"All right!" He looked at Tower and then at the rest of the men, one by one. "All right," he repeated in a quieter tone. "There'll be no cover-up, I assure you, but we'll keep this matter among ourselves for the time being. No leaks to newspapermen, or anybody else, or somebody's head will be on the block along with Dondero's! And I want that Sergeant Dondero! I want him bad! I hate a bad cop! We'll get him, and we'll get his side of the story, and he'll be called upon to answer charges to the department as well as all criminal charges." He looked around the room for one last time. "All right, that's it! Get this Dondero!"

Sure, Reardon thought sourly as he filed from the room with the rest; get this Dondero. Whatever happened to the original scenario, he wondered—get Pop Holland?

Monday—2:00 P.M.

Reardon turned the Charger south into Van Ness, drove a few blocks, and then was halted by a traffic light. He stared up at the red glow without consciously seeing it, thinking back on all the places he had stopped that morning, every place he could think of in connection with Dondero—girl friends' apartments, several of them; several bowling alleys the two men had bowled at together; a pool hall he knew was a favorite of Dondero's; restaurants where he and Jan and Don and his current date had eaten; places Dondero had mentioned in passing, as enjoying the food—

A blast of a horn from behind reminded him the light had changed. He stepped on the gas and found himself driving past Tommy's Joynt. Speaking of food, he thought, and stepped precipitously on the brake; there was another angry blast of a horn and a taxi swerved around him, its driver waving a fist. Reardon paid it no attention and angled in to the curb. While Tommy's Joynt was not one of the places that Dondero normally frequented, it still served food, and Reardon suddenly remembered he had had neither breakfast nor lunch. He glanced at his watch and was surprised to see how late it was. Well, he thought, with the schedule I've been keeping lately, my stomach probably thinks my watch has been stolen, anyway, so let's get a sandwich and an ale and surprise the old intestine.

At that hour, after the luncheon crowd and before the supper crowd, Tommy's Joynt was reasonably empty. Reardon approached the pile of trays and was about to remove one when he felt a tap on his arm. He turned, frowning in surprise, and found a busboy studying him a bit apprehensively.

"Your name Reardon?"

"That's right. Why?"

"Telephone," the busboy said, relieved that he had not disturbed a stranger for nothing. "Guy described you and said you just walked in, but you know that don't always mean too much—"

"Yeah," Reardon said, and walked to the telephone on the wall beneath the small balcony. He couldn't imagine who on earth might have guessed he would be in Tommy's Joynt at that hour, but then decided maybe somebody was trying every eatery in town, and had just struck it lucky. He picked up the dangling receiver. "Reardon," he said shortly.

"Ah, Lieutenant! We meet again, if again only verbally." Reardon's jaw tightened at the familiar, slightly amused voice, but then he knew that subconsciously he had known the call was probably from the kidnapper. Who else seemed to be omnipotent? The voice went on smoothly. "I thought you'd never stop in one place long enough for me to get in touch with you. A place with a single telephone, that is. But hunger finally got you, and I'm pleased."

Reardon glanced swiftly at the doorway. Somewhere very near, maybe even watching the front of Tommy's Joynt as he spoke, was the man he wanted. But he also knew that it would be useless to drop the phone and dash into the street. There were endless telephones within a block of that busy corner, in stores, motels, hotels, gas stations. He dropped the idea, concentrating instead on the call.

"What do you want?"

"Just an apology this time, Lieutenant." The deep voice actually sounded apologetic. "Sorry about Lazaretti, but you see, it was just a terrible mistake. A dreadful one, really, and so needless! Poor Lazaretti. Didn't even speak English, you know. Ah, well, that's water over the dam, I'm afraid. I'm also afraid," the voice went on, now losing its apologetic tone, "that now we shall have to trouble you for the other one. Patrone, I believe his name is. Tonight at two in the morning, same place, same drill. And, by the way, since I'm sure you're interested, Sergeant Holland is doing as well as can be expected. He's a bleeder, did you know? I don't know how he'd tolerate any further operations . . ."

There was a trailing off of the last words; when the receiver was placed back on the hook it was done so quietly that for a moment Reardon didn't realize he had been disconnected.

He hung up and walked to the open door of the restaurant, staring out into the street. Somewhere out there, within yards of him, was the man who had kidnapped Pop and mutilated him. And trying to find him by staring out at the usual activity of the busy corner was pointless. Especially since all he had to go on was the man's voice, and not another thing. He turned back and walked to the food counter. He knew he supposedly should be returning instantly to the Hall to report the call, but he had to eat somewhere and he might as well do it while he had the chance. He picked up a tray, loaded it with the necessary utensils, and started down the deserted line, thinking hard.

For one thing, he had definitely been followed all morning, and for all he knew, he might well have been followed for some time. Still, since he hadn't been paying any attention to that possibility, trying to remember who might have been watching him could only lead to invention, so it was better to drop that angle at once. From now on, of course, it would be well to try and keep an eye on any potential follower, but the chances were he would be left alone in the future. This man didn't seem to do much of anything the same way twice.

A more important thought intruded. He had always known, of course, that Dondero had removed Lazaretti from custody only to effect the trade for Pop, and that he had nothing to do with any torture, but it was still nice to have it confirmed. What, then, had been the exact timing of events? One o'clock Dondero takes the prisoner from the Hall—

Reardon became aware he was being addressed. He looked up.

"Yes?"

The counterman was eying him with curiosity. "You buying, mister, or just window-shopping?"

"Oh." Reardon came down to earth. "I'm buying." He surveyed the wealth of succulent viands spread out in the various hot trays, trying to make up his mind. He'd had beef the last time he'd been here, that time with Porky, and it had been very good. And speaking of Porky, the ribs looked inviting. But he'd been eating a lot of fatty foods lately, and Jan had this thing about cholesterol, so maybe—

"Hey!" The counterman was frowning at him. "What do you want, Mac? A estimate?"

"No, I'll have the fish—"

Reardon stopped, wrinkling his forehead, as the word triggered an entire series of tiny electronic flashes in his brain. Fish, by God! Of course! That was it! The counterman paused in the process of transferring a fillet onto a plate and peered at his customer wonderingly, disturbed by the sudden grimace that crossed the other's face.

"Hey, Mac, you all right?"

"Fish, by God!" Reardon said triumphantly, and abandoned his tray, moving toward the open door of the Joynt at a half-trot.

The counterman stared after the running figure a moment with a puzzled frown; then he shrugged and slid the fillet back to join its brothers in the hot tray. "Three-dollar bill," he said to no one in particular, and then whistled shrilly for the busboy to come and remove the deserted tray before it interfered with normal traffic.

Monday—3:10 P.M.

The narrow half-twisted and falling-apart dock lay under the hot September sun like a long wounded wooden animal, resting before resuming its struggle to straighten itself out. Reardon, walking its precarious length and trying to avoid the rotting planks, paused at the end, pleased to have made it, and looked down at the broad-beamed little fishing boat bobbing placidly there. Across the bay the hills of San Lorenzo and Hayward could be seen, shimmering through the afternoon haze, small buildings dotting their sides. But here, south of Burlingame, hidden in the reeds, one might have been on a deserted island. A bluebottle fly approached to appraise the interloper; Reardon brushed it away impatiently, studied the deserted deck a moment, and then raised his voice.

"Dondero!"

There was a faint echo as his voice came back to him from across the water. He wondered if his hunch might have been wrong after all, and then called again.

"Hey, Dondero!"

Dondero's tousled and sleepy head appeared in the shadowed square that marked the small companionway. He yawned deeply, grinned at Reardon in a slightly embarrassed manner, and scratched at the T-shirt that covered his hairy chest.

"Hi, Jim. You woke me up." He looked down the dock toward the land. "No escort?"

"I figured without an escort you'd confess faster," Reardon said, and added more soberly, "anyway, when you told me about this fishing boat, you asked me to keep it to myself."

"So I did. I didn't feel I wanted every cop in San Francisco figuring this would make a dandy place for weekend picnics, for him and his fourteen kids," Dondero said. He looked toward land again, studying the Charger parked all alone on the jetty. "Still, under the circumstances, there was a good chance you'd purposely forget. However . . ." He yawned. "Well, now you're here, come on down and have a beer."

"You bring them up," Reardon suggested. "It looks warm down there."

Dondero looked at him a long moment. Then he said, "Yeah, it's warm down there, all right. And I've got a machine gun all set up down there for snooping intruders. Sure you want to drink on duty?"

"Just get the beer."

"Right," Dondero said, and disappeared from view. He reappeared a moment later with two cans of beer, each dripping with sweat. He handed one to Reardon, swung himself up to seat himself on the rickety dock, and looked up. "Hold up on the handcuffs until I get this down, will you?"

"I don't know." Reardon sat down beside the other man and pulled the tab free from his can. The cold liquid felt and tasted good going down. He took another protracted drink, rested the empty can on his knee, and looked at Dondero evenly. "I ought to arrest you for stupidity, if for nothing else. Going to tell me about it?"

Dondero grinned a bit sheepishly and shrugged.

"What's to tell? Two o'clock tomorrow morning, if everything works out, the man lets Pop Holland go, and I go back into circulation." He took a draught of his beer and stared across the bay. "Oh, I expect I'll get my share of flak for pulling the guy out of the cell block, but I figure the brass won't be too hard-mouthed about it if Pop's okay and it all works out."

Reardon set his empty can to one side. "And if it doesn't work out?"

"Why shouldn't it work out?"

"I mean just what I said. Suppose the chief, and the Board of Commissioners and even Captain Clark—God save the mark!— are right, and the brilliant Sergeant Dondero is wrong?"

"Wrong in what way?"

"Wrong in every way," Reardon said firmly. "For starters, suppose the guy doesn't let Pop go?"

Dondero shrugged. "Why shouldn't he? But supposing he don't —what have we lost? What difference does it make if this Lazaretti is walking the streets? If we want him back, when the man gets through with him, he'll be easy enough to pick up; and if he's blown town, so much the better. There'll be one less so-called tough guy around to make trouble. So what's the problem?"

Reardon figured Dondero was certainly innocent. Not, he reminded himself, that he had ever had any doubts, even before the telephone call he had received at Tommy's Joynt.

"The problem is—"

"The problem is," Dondero interrupted, "that all you guys think Pop's dead and I released a prisoner for nothing. Then where does that leave Sergeant Dondero? In the soup, I admit." He shook his head. "Only I don't think Pop's dead. I think Pop's very much alive, and I'm damned if I'm going to sit around and watch him get hurt, Board of Commissioners or not. Not when all it takes to get him free is to trade off a midget meathead like Lazaretti. It'll work out, Jim. Don't worry."

"No," Reardon said quietly. "It won't work out."

Dondero frowned. "You sound like you know something I don't."

Reardon nodded somberly.

"Yes, I do. I know that Lazaretti was fished out of the bay early this morning, about six. Somebody did a job on him with fire—matches, a lighted candle—undoubtedly to get him to talk about something, but whether or not he talked before he died we don't know."

Dondero was staring at him, his beer forgotten.

"As a matter of fact," Reardon continued, his tone without expression, "the consensus down at the Hall is that you were the one who was holding those matches—"

"What!"

"That's right," Reardon said in the same even tone. "They think that since you were unable to get the information you wanted from Lazaretti up in the 'conference room,' you took him outside and worked him over. They figure he died on you, most likely before you could get any useful information from him, so you dumped him in the bay and now you're on the run."

Dondero had been listening unbelievingly. Now he took a deep breath and let it out slowly.

"They got to be crazy! They got to be completely out of their so-called minds!" A thought came to him. "You don't think any nutty thing like that, do you, Jim?"

"No," Reardon said quietly, "I don't think so, and I'll tell you why. I had a call while I was having lunch—or about to have lunch, now that I remember—and it was from the man who's holding Pop. He admitted to having knocked off Lazaretti—"

"So no wonder you had so much faith in me!" Dondero said witheringly.

"Sure. Why else? Anyway, the man said he hadn't wanted Lazaretti in the first place. He had made a terrible mistake. From the way he spoke, it appeared there was a certain lack of communication between him and Lazaretti, among other things. What he wants, now, he says, is the other one. Patrone, or whatever his name is."

"It's Patrone." Dondero considered the situation and sighed disconsolately. "Man, I really screwed up this time, didn't I?"

116

"Like a champ," Reardon said with honesty. "Given twenty years' practice, I doubt you could have screwed up any better. However, there's a bright side, if you want to look at it—"

"What's that?"

"You can't get up into the cell blocks and release Patrone, thank God! Zelinski would be waiting for you."

"Very funny," Dondero said sourly. He finished his beer, looked at the can in his hand a moment as if wondering how it got there, and then tossed it moodily into the bay. Just thinking about all his problems was enough to depress anyone, so he picked up Reardon's can from the dock and tossed it in after his own, for luck. "Trouble, trouble!" he said bitterly. "Why did I ever learn Italian at my mother's knee? Why didn't I learn Esperanto, like everyone else? Why didn't I—"

He paused suddenly, struck by a beautiful thought.

"Hey!"

Reardon looked at him. "Hey, what?"

Dondero thought about his beautiful thought a bit longer, but could find nothing wrong with it. "Wait a second! You said this guy said he made a mistake in wanting Lazaretti?"

"Those were practically his exact words."

"Tell me what he said, will you? As close as you can remember? Exactly?"

Reardon frowned. Dondero was deadly serious.

"All right," he said slowly. "He said he was sorry he'd killed Lazaretti, that it was a terrible mistake, 'a dreadful one' were his exact words. Then he said it was water over the dam, but that he was afraid now he would have to trouble us for the other one, Patrone, he said he believed his name was. He added the exchange was to be at two o'clock, same place, same drill, added to that that Pop Holland was a bleeder, and hung up." He studied Dondero's exultant expression with curiosity. "Why?"

Dondero was grinning savagely.

"Sure!" he said triumphantly. "That's it! I should have seen it sooner!"

"See what?"

"You know something, Jim? That character never saw either Lazaretti or Patrone in person in his entire life!"

117

"Maybe not," Reardon said, totally unimpressed. "So what?"

"So lots of things, don't you see?" Dondero was getting more excited by the minute. "If he doesn't know Patrone by sight, he sure as hell won't know if the guy he picks up at the bridge tonight *isn't* Patrone, will he?" He answered his own question. "No, ma'am, he will not!"

Reardon studied his friend for several moments as the meaning of the other's words slowly sank in. Then he shook his head forcefully.

"No way, buster!"

"Why not?" Dondero said aggressively, liking his idea more and more by the minute. "Hell, I speak Italian like a native—"

"Lazaretti also spoke Italian like a native."

"Hey, that's right! Wait a second—" Dondero snapped his fingers. "You said he had a communication problem with Lazaretti. Five gets you ten that Lazaretti didn't speak English, and that Patrone does! I won't even need my Italian; my superb English will do. I—"

"Cut it out," Reardon said sternly. "It's just a wild guess the man doesn't know Patrone on sight—"

"He doesn't, I tell you! Would he have made a mistake in which guy he wanted out, if he knew one from the other? Or knew either one from a hole in the wall? He hasn't a clue—"

"I said, cut it out! This man plays rough. He killed Lazaretti, and he wasn't neat about it, either. And he cut off one of Pop's fingers. He's got his hands on one cop, and that's one too many. He wants answers, and maybe this Patrone knows those answers or maybe he doesn't, but it's damn sure you don't even know the questions!"

"So there's one sure way to find out what those questions are," Dondero said logically. "That's to keep your big fat ears open when the man asks them; right? Anyway," he pointed out, "I'm in the doghouse so far by this time, the only way I can come out is through the other end. If I come up with something real bright, maybe the brass won't do any more than hang me."

"Except for lots of things—"

"Such as?"

"Well," Reardon said, thinking about it, "in addition to all the hundreds of other objections, let's take just one. Let's suppose the man picks you up where he says, when he says—"

"Yeah."

"And he takes you to wherever he plans to take you after he picks you up—"

"Yeah."

"And when you get there, he takes you into this room—"

"Yeah."

"And Pop is sitting there, and Pop says, 'Hello, Don, so you guys finally got here, huh?' "

"Now, wait a second," Dondero said hastily. "It won't work like that at all. To begin with, there's no reason why this character should introduce me to Pop—I'd think he'd want to keep us apart. I don't imagine he's out to advertise he kidnapped a cop, especially not to some character he just sprung from jail." He thought about it a moment more, and then shook his head. "No, that's the least of my worries."

"If that's the *least* of your worries—"

But Dondero was not listening. He was already back with his planning.

"I've got a black suit just like the one Lazaretti had on, I use it for weddings and funerals, and I've got a whole hamper full of dirty white shirts, all we have to do is take out the label—"

Reardon felt himself being drawn into the scheme despite himself. "Except we've got a man on your apartment."

"But he wouldn't stop *you*," Dondero pointed out, and went on before Reardon could say anything. "The suit's hanging—"

"Now, wait a second!"

Dondero looked at him a long moment. "I started to say, the suit's hanging in the front closet," he said quietly. When Reardon remained silent, Dondero smiled faintly and went on. "As I say, we'll have to take out all the labels, and probably get it wrinkled and dirty, which is no chore, since I should have sent it to the cleaners months ago. The shirts are in the hamper in the bathroom. I've got an old pair of black shoes here on the boat that ought to do. I'll manage to get any maker's name off them, although I doubt he'll be down on the floor peeking at my booties—"

"Look," Reardon said desperately, and ran his hand through his hair. "If we're really going to do this insane thing, then it has to be properly planned, and I can't think clearly on an empty stomach. What do you have to eat on this bucket?"

"What?"

"Eat. Food. Vitamins and minerals." Reardon motioned toward his mouth with bunched fingers. "What kind of Italian are you, you don't read simple sign language?"

"The word's *mangiare*," Dondero said loftily, and jumped down to the slanted deck. "Well, come on, then, although I'm damned if I can figure out how you ever manage to solve a case, when all you can think about is your stomach!"

CHAPTER 10

Tuesday—1:05 A.M.

Fog was beginning to sweep up from the bay as Reardon bumped down the rutted lane leading from the main road to the jetty and the dock mooring Dondero's small fisherman; a light drizzle was attempting to dissipate the mist and managed only to compound the general unpleasantness of the night. Reardon kicked himself for having left both umbrella and raincoat at home, pulled the car around to face the way he had come in, and turned off the ignition. He flicked the lights to the parking position, stared out at the rain for a moment, and then ducked from the car with his bundle, holding it over his head for as much protection as possible. He made his way down the precarious length of the dilapidated slippery dock, amost going into the water several times, and finally reached his goal, cursing loud, long, and fluently. As if in response, the hatchway was opened and light angled up from below, losing itself at once in the sodden night.

"About goddamn time!" Reardon muttered savagely under his breath, and dropped to the pitching deck of the small fishing boat, feeling it heel under his weight.

Dondero was watching him with a smile. "I heard you give the password. Advance, friend. Hey, you got the stuff!" His smile faded. "It isn't wrapped. It'll be all wet."

"Yeah." Reardon climbed down the narrow companionway after Dondero, happy to be out of the rain, but still not overjoyed to be involved in the idiotic scheme at all. He tossed the damp bundle onto one of the two bunks that lined the outer bulkheads of the small cabin, walked over to the head and helped himself to a towel, vigorously wiping his head with it. "You'll probably be wetter after tonight if you go through with this ridiculous idea," he said darkly. "Probably a lot wetter," he added ominously, "when we fish you out of the bay."

"You're just trying to make me feel good," Dondero said. He was unfolding the bundle. "You're just mad because you didn't think of the idea yourself." He shook out a wrinkled dirty white shirt that had been at the bundle's core and slipped it on over his undershirt, buttoning it up to the collar. He considered himself in the mirror. "I've got a picture of my great-grandfather taken somewhere in the Abruzzi when he was a young man, and he wasn't wearing a tie, either. Now I know where I get my good looks."

He kicked off his sneakers, slipped out of his dungarees, and pulled on the trousers of his black silk suit. He started to bring up the zipper and suddenly cringed.

Reardon looked at the other's grimace unsympathetically. "What's the matter? Catch yourself?"

"No, they're wet! Why the hell didn't you at least leave the pants on the inside?" He pulled on the jacket and studied himself in the mirror. He turned to Reardon for approbation. "How do I look?"

"Like your great-grandfather. All ready to be laid out." Reardon bent to a small cabinet beneath the cabin's desk, brought out a bottle of brandy, and lifted a glass from one of the gimbal-type holders there. He straightened up, poured himself a generous drink, and took it down in one gulp. He gasped and stared at the bottle. "Good God! Where did you get this stuff? What is it? Fermented bay water?"

"You have no taste," Dondero said with the air of a connoisseur. He bent down, brought up another glass, and reached for the bottle, but Reardon took the glass from his hand, setting it down on the desk.

"Are you intent on committing suicide? He'd smell the liquor on your breath. We don't give prisoners brandy before releasing them, and we don't stop at bars with them on the way to trading them for sergeants. It isn't regulations." He looked at the bottle and wrinkled his nose. "Anyway, we don't give prisoners this kind of brandy, or they'd have us up on cruelty charges."

"If you hate it so much, quit polishing it off," Dondero said. He dropped down on one of the bunks and slid into his shoes, reaching down to tie them. He straightened up and looked at his watch. "How much time before we have to leave?"

"About five minutes," Reardon said. "And give me that watch. We also don't furnish prisoners with timepieces before trading them for sergeants; anyway, not Timex watches, made in America."

"I forgot. Anyway, they probably sell Timex in Italy, too, or Patrone could have bought it here. If I really wanted to take the part of an Italian visitor, I ought to be wearing about six of them." But he still took off the watch and handed it to Reardon, and then stared down at his hands. Then he stood up and studied himself in the mirror again. "Not bad. I hope." He glanced over his shoulder. "Incidentally, how did you get the stuff out of the apartment?"

"Johnny Merchant was watching the place. I told him I was going to shake the joint down. Since we had no instructions to break in, and since we had no warrant—and since Johnny is a smart cop—he went around the corner for a beer while I went through the closets." Reardon shrugged. "The stuff was in my car, stuffed down behind the seat, when he came back."

Dondero's preoccupation momentarily took a back seat to his admiration.

"You know," he said, "you'd make a great criminal, James. Remind me not to leave any valuables around the apartment from now on." He started to look at his wristwatch and then remembered he didn't have it. "Hey, let's get going, huh?"

"If you insist," Reardon said, and poured himself one for the road. Dondero was getting a bit up-tight sitting around, and if he was going through with his idiotic scheme, at least he shouldn't be allowed to get overly worked up ahead of time. Reardon slugged the drink down, grimaced again at the taste, and went to the companionway ladder. "Up we go."

Dondero grunted and followed. He paused long enough to lock the hatchway cover and then made his way behind Reardon down the length of the convoluted dock to the jetty. Reardon splashed through the puddles to the Charger, ducked inside hastily, and leaned over to unlock the opposite door. Dondero clambered inside, slammed the door shut behind him, and wiped water from his face.

"And I'm going to stand out on an open bridge in this weather waiting for somebody to pick me up?"

"As you've been so fond of saying—this was your bright idea."

"Yeah. I got to be crazy, huh? What a night!" He tried to peer through the window and gave up. "Man, I don't care if this guy's picking me up in a boat, or a car, or a helicopter—I hope whatever it is has a roof, is all."

Reardon looked at him. "You can still change your mind."

"Change it for what?"

Reardon studied the set face a moment and then started the engine. Dondero's mind was made up, and it was apparent in the hard jaw and narrowed eyes. Reardon sighed and put up the headlights; he started the windshield wipers and defroster, and started to drive down the muddy lane toward the main road. He bumped over the curb into the highway, checked in both directions for traffic, and started the long drive toward the city, leaning back and trying to wriggle into a more comfortable position in his wet clothes.

"Incidentally, I saw Patrone this evening," he said conversationally.

"Oh?" Dondero was looking at him expectantly.

"He's a little bigger than Lazaretti, but not all that much. A little smaller than you."

"And needs a shave like me, I hope," Dondero said with a grin, and rubbed a hand over his own stubble.

"And needs a shave like you do, and like Lazaretti did," Reardon said. His eyes were steady on the deserted, rainy road; his hands steady on the wheel. "And you were right. He speaks English."

124

"I'm always right—"

"Except when you get bright ideas. Anyway, my guess is when he was pretending not to speak English, it was probably just to be hard-nosed with Zelinski." He smiled. "Which almost puts me on his side."

"Me, too."

"He tried to pull the same routine on me, only before I even saw him I took the trouble to call Rome and talk to some police captain there. He checked for me, and Patrone's got a sheet. Nothing major; nothing to stop him from getting and holding a passport. Small-time stuff. He used to make his living escorting visiting Americans around Rome—which is difficult if you don't speak English—and every now and then, according to the cops there, servicing some of the lonely American ladies—"

"Hey, hey!" Dondero said. "Do you suppose this character wants Patrone out of jail to service a lonely lady?"

"You can hope so, anyway," Reardon said dryly. "At any rate, the cops there have a pretty good idea Patrone used to augment his income by picking up tips from pocketbooks on bedroom dressers without his patroness of the day knowing she was being so generous. Only one really raised a stink, but she had no proof as to how much she had in her purse when she went to bed, so Patrone walked out free and clear."

"Our boy's a bum," Dondero said disappointedly. "A small-time bum."

"Who did you hope you were impersonating?" Reardon glanced across the car. "The head of the Italian CIA?"

"No, but a plain bum—"

"Well," Reardon said, "maybe he's a bum, but he was a bum smart enough to con some American ladies."

"What's that mean? Look at how many American ladies you've conned. Hey!" Dondero suddenly said, struck by another of his brilliant ideas. "Maybe that's it! Maybe this guy who's holding Pop, maybe Patrone conned his wife, or his girl friend. Maybe he took her to bed—"

"And for this, this guy goes to the trouble of kidnapping a policeman—and mutilating him—and killing a second man?"

"Well," Dondero said, still intrigued by the idea, "you know how some guys are about their dames, and about revenge. . . ."

Through the rain and the darkness a glow against the sky ahead marked the location of the San Francisco International Airport. Reardon glanced at his watch in the light from the dashboard. Still ample time. He went back to Dondero's statement.

"I only know how I am about revenge," he said, wondering if what he was saying was accurate or only an answer to Dondero's presentation. "If I wanted revenge on some street guide in Rome, I think I'd take a plane to Rome and look up this street guide, and do something about it. I doubt if I'd sit in San Francisco, here, and wait for the man to conveniently show up. He just might not do it."

"Well, maybe not," Dondero said grudgingly. He hated to see a good theory go down the drain, especially one of his own. "Maybe we'll know more about it after tonight."

"Yes," Reardon said quietly. "I certainly hope to God we do!"

Dondero seemed to find something significant in Reardon's tone. He frowned.

"I don't like the way you said that, Jim."

"You don't like the way I said what?" Reardon looked hurt. "All I said was, 'I hope we will.' What's wrong with that?"

"Nothing's wrong with that," Dondero said quietly, "only that's not exactly what you said. To me, it sounded like we were back on the same argument we had this afternoon. It sounded like you were right back with some screwy idea of trying to follow me tonight."

"Who, me?"

"Yeah!" Dondero said, now convinced. "And when you give me that 'Who, me?' routine, I'm more convinced than ever." He glared across the darkened interior of the car. "Look, you wouldn't even let me slide a beeper down my pants like I wanted—"

"If they found it on you," Reardon said flatly, "you'd be dead in five minutes. And Pop, too."

"And if they find Lieutenant James Reardon, my bosom buddy

—who they have demonstrated they know inside and out—on my tail, what then? What rebate do I get on my insurance premium then, pal?" He shook his head violently. "No, damn it! If you want to play Lone Ranger, do it on somebody else's horse! Drop me off, like the man wants, and then go about your business. Go to a movie, or go home and take a cold shower, but don't—please! —don't try and be cute and follow me." His voice became plaintive. "Damn it, Jim, I thought we went all over that this afternoon!"

Either the fog was getting thicker or the rain more dense, or South San Francisco was economizing on its electricity bill, Reardon thought, because the blackness continued to stretch on either side of the highway. It was like driving through an endless tunnel. The kidnapper, whoever he was, was luckier than he deserved to be, to get weather like this tonight! Or maybe not . . .

"That was this afternoon," Reardon said slowly. "I've been thinking—on a night like this I could follow you and never be seen." He checked his watch in the light from the dashboard and nodded. He gestured with one hand toward his two-way radio. "As a matter of fact, we could even be a few minutes late and I could probably raise Stan, or Ferguson—they're both on nights; it wouldn't take long—and we could cover you like a tent. They could cover Third Street from each side, down a side street nobody could see, and I could even probably get the Harbor Patrol to have a boat around, in case they pick you up that way—"

"No!"

"They've got these night binoculars that cut right through this garbage weather—"

"No! Damn it, how many times do I have to say it? NO!" Dondero changed his tone, turning to pleading. "Jim, please. Don't help me. Don't even *try* to help me. Eighty-seven and a half per cent of all the trouble in this world comes from people trying to help other people. That's a reliable statistic."

"That's a great attitude for a cop."

"At the moment I'm not a cop. I'm an Italian fugitive named Patrone who just got let out of jail for reasons he can't fathom, and if you don't blow as soon as you drop me off, I'll probably end up being a dead Italian fugitive named Patrone! Who still won't know why he's being sprung. . . ."

"Nobody followed Lazaretti," Reardon pointed out, "and look where he is."

"I'm not Lazaretti; I'm Patrone. And nobody followed Pop Holland, and look where he is," Dondero said stubbornly. "Besides, Lazaretti didn't know the answers the man wanted."

"And you do?"

"I'm a better bluffer," Dondero said aggressively, and lapsed into silence.

Reardon sighed and appeared to concede. The city had mysteriously sprung up about them as they had driven, and they were approaching the intersection of Route 101 with Bayshore, and the turnoff to Third Street; he wanted to concentrate all his attention on the scene. Somewhere off to his right, he knew, was an empty, deserted Candlestick Park, but all he could see when he glanced in that direction was a wall of wet mist.

He slowed down and turned into the Third Street exit. A careening automobile swung past him, startling him by its sudden appearance, drenching the Charger with water and then disappearing into the night, its taillight fading quickly in the fog and rain. It made Reardon realize how easily one could allow the night to hide one, if one was courageous enough to drive without lights of any kind. True, one might run over an embankment, or into a telephone pole, but at least he would do it invisibly. He glanced into the rear-view mirror, saw nothing but mist, and brought his attention back to the roadway.

Through the fog the faint outlines of small houses crowding the side streets in working-class land economy could barely be seen, and then they were lost to sight as the fog swirled up. The lampposts edged by, one by one, until there, ahead, the bridge over the channel could suddenly be seen under a pair of overhead hooded lamps, swinging in the wind and rain. Reardon started to slow down when he thought of something.

"Don, what if he doesn't show up?"

"Then I'll catch my death of cold and they won't have to fire me off the force," Dondero said with a cheerfulness he was far from feeling. He stared through the blurred windshield and his voice turned bitter. "Why in hell wasn't Patrone wearing a raincoat when he was picked up?" He saw the bridge ahead and his voice tightened a bit despite himself. "All right, here we are. Stop the car and heave me out like the man would expect a good cop to do."

Reardon obediently brought the car to a halt in the center of the bridge, reached across Dondero's body, and opened the door. His hand appeared to be aiding Dondero in descending, but in reality he was squeezing the other man's arm tightly for good luck. "Take care," he said under his breath. "Get lost," Dondero replied, equally quietly, and then the door was closing behind him and Reardon was driving off into the darkness of the night, his wheels spraying water on either side.

He drove slowly, as a man would in weather like this, his eyes searching the darkness of the street's shoulder for any sign of an occupied car, or an approaching vehicle which might be coming to pick Dondero up, but there was nothing for him to see, and his rear-view mirror revealed nothing in that downpour. It was probably a boat, he thought, as they had considered. He thought again of calling the Harbor Patrol, and then decided against it. It was one thing for him to take on the responsibility of following Dondero, if the man coming for him was coming by road, but it was quite another thing to let the responsibility fall into other hands. Other hands might, without meaning to, do something sufficiently suspicious to lead to harm for Dondero. The same held true of Ferguson, or Stan Lundahl, or any of the others. This was something he'd have to do himself, and he knew he had known it ever since he had agreed to the scheme.

He came to Army and passed it without diminishing his speed. He would swing around at the next block, assuming he didn't see anything in the meantime, and start back slowly; then pull off at the small road just this side of the bridge, his lights out. Anyone coming for Don would certainly not be coming from that direction, not down a dead-end street, and he should be able to pick them up and follow them, using their taillights for a guide.

He turned into the next street, backed out swiftly, and started back down Third Street at the same even speed, thinking. In a way, Dondero was right; to follow could easily lead to disaster. Still, not to follow was unthinkable. The entire idea was what was basically wrong. Even as the thought came, another followed, one he knew to be correct and certain. The thing to do was not to follow anyone, and not to have anyone to follow. The proper thing to do was to get back to the bridge as soon as possible, pick Don up if he had to pull him into the car by his ears, and let the brains at the Hall decide what was really the right thing to do after that!

His mind made up, and satisfied that he had come to the right decision, even though tardily, he stepped on the gas, the car swaying along, shoving water from under the tires in steady spurts. He glanced at his watch and then instantly back to the road, surprised he hadn't lost control even in that split second. It was still a minute or two before two o'clock; they wouldn't have come for Don yet. He must have been insane ever to let Don talk him into the stupid idea in the first place.

No car had passed in either direction since he had swung around; in fact, he had seen no car at all on the road since that crazy character off Route 101. And they would never attempt using a boat on the bay in that weather; the best bay captain in the world would be docked tonight, and not taking any chance in that garbage of being sunk by a tug, or another of those hooting monsters out there. As a matter of fact, the chances were the deep-voiced sardonic bastard would simply forget the whole thing on a night like this. He'd probably postpone it until the following night, and probably manage a message, one way or another, to that effect once everyone had gotten soaked to the skin! What a system!

He crossed Army, his speed dangerously high, his eyes alert for any other car, but there were none. The streetlamps fled past; the overhead swinging arcs making the entrance to the small bridge appeared suddenly out of the dark. He slowed down, his eyes searching the gloom for Dondero, a smile quirking his lips at the thought of the half-drowned detective. It would serve him right, getting bright ideas!

His headlights rose as he hit the bridge, his foot pressing insistently on the brake; then they dipped, sweeping the entire expanse.

The bridge was empty. Dondero was gone.

CHAPTER 11

Tuesday–1:58 A.M.

Dondero turned his collar up against the rain and watched the taillights of Reardon's Charger disappear in the fog and darkness in the direction of the Embarcadero and the center of the city. He tried to put aside any thought of his discomfort, concentrating instead on what a real fugitive would do, Italian or otherwise, if the police—for mysterious reasons of their own, not explained to a prisoner—took him to some unfamiliar place on a miserable night like this, and kicked him out of the car. Well, his first thought, quite naturally, would be to expect a gun blast to cut him down, and when this didn't occur he would probably take the next second or two thanking his saints he hadn't been brought here to be assassinated, in the manner of some cops in some countries.

After that, the fugitive would probably waste another second wondering why, then, he had been taken there at all. And after that, there is no doubt at all as to what he would do: he would get out of there as fast as he could, and leave the mystery of his release to be explained another time.

He would not know that a person was scheduled to meet him; he most probably would also not know of Lazaretti's death—although the prison telegraph system was remarkable, and a lot better than Western Union, as what wasn't; so he would merely assume his release was either an administrative error, or that some unknown friend had greased a few palms. But after spending a maximum of five seconds cerebrating the above, he'd get the hell out of there.

With that final conclusion reached in even less than five seconds, Dondero took one swift look about him and then started off in the direction Reardon's car had taken. He had taken exactly one squishy step when he realized he was not alone.

"Hold it!"

There was something about the authority of the voice which, though the words were not delivered in overly loud tones, sounded familiar to him as a cop, and would even have been recognizable to him in his role of Italian fugitive. It was the authority of someone with a weapon to back up that authority, and even if Patrone hadn't spoken English, he would have known what was required of him, just from the tone. Dondero stopped abruptly, waiting, staring in the direction he thought the voice had come from. Then, almost to his relief, he saw the small shape near one corner of the bridge; as his eyes adjusted to the dark he saw that it was a small man with a very large hat and a raincoat that dropped almost to the ground. In that light he almost looked like a large tree stump on which someone had deposited a large hat. Dondero eyed the hat enviously; it was almost as good as an umbrella. He had brought his hands up almost automatically at the command; now he was about to drop them when he saw, extending from the tree stump, a large revolver, apparently taken from beneath the raincoat. Dondero, having been expecting it, was not surprised.

"Over here."

Dondero shrugged. He had wanted to be picked up, so why be coy about it? Anyway, if he remained where he was very long, he figured the chances were he'd drown. He walked toward the small figure, but as he approached it, it seemed to recede; then he saw that the small man had merely stepped back and was now walking down a narrow path that paralleled the channel in the direction of the bay, looking back over his shoulder with his revolver ever ready.

"Follow me, but not too close."

133

Dondero followed along. He stumbled over something, realized at the last moment that it was a railroad rail, and was more careful in crossing its companion. They were in a weed-filled area, with the grit of cinders beneath their feet, walking past empty boxcars; what little could be discerned of them in the darkness indicated they had been abandoned years before. Dondero suddenly realized it was a spur of the S.P.R.R. he had thought torn out years before; he was going to have to keep up on his geography of the city if he was going to know where he was being kidnapped in the future, because he would have sworn that there was nothing but empty fields between Third and the bay in this area.

He slogged on, the cinders underfoot giving way to mud, the wet weeds slapping at his thighs, soaking him to the skin. Ahead of him the little man moved steadily, the gun held in readiness. A fourth shadowed boxcar was passed when he noticed the little man had stopped and was motioning him forward with the gun.

"Over here."

There was a car parked there, almost invisible, paralleling a boxcar and almost touching it. In that darkness and fog it would be well out of sight of anyone on Third Street, Dondero realized, and then thought it would probably be equally invisible from Third Street on a bright, sunny, day. He approached the car, his main consideration being that it represented shelter from the weather, but when he reached for the door handle, he felt the gun jabbed into his ribs. He winced.

"Hey! What that for?"

"Lean against the car."

"All you got to do is ask." Dondero hoped his harsh gutteral was an approximation of Patrone's voice; he also hoped his captor was as unfamiliar as he was with the extent of English possessed by street guides in Rome. Still, being searched was only to be expected, although what they thought the police allowed prisoners to carry with them when being traded would make interesting conjecture. Well, he had on him what Lazaretti had on him when he had dropped the other man off at the bridge the night before, and that was nothing. He leaned against the car, feet apart, as if he were quite accustomed to both the position and to being

134

searched. A small hand fanned him expertly; then the small man stepped back.

"Okay. Inside."

Dondero climbed in, pleased finally to be out of the terrible weather. The door across from him opened and the small man got in, preceded by the raised gun. He held the gun on Dondero steadily while he closed the door and fumbled in one pocket of the raincoat, producing a pair of handcuffs.

"Slip these through the armrest and cuff yourself."

"I don' unnerstand." Dondero prayed to his ancestors for forgiveness for his stage-Italian accent. He glowered at the little man. "Who you? Why dose cops, dey take me out of jail and put me down out dere in all dat rain, huh? What goes on, huh? What you want from me? Who are you?" Listening to himself, Dondero thought he sounded more like a stage-French Canadian, rather than an Italian, and could only hope the little man was no expert in linguistics.

"I'm a friend," the little man said quietly, "just as long as you behave yourself and do what you're told. Now, put the cuffs through the door handle and cuff yourself, and don't pretend you don't know what I'm talking about, because if I've got to translate any more, I'd just as soon shoot you. Not kill you, friend, because George wouldn't like that; just shoot you where you won't be cantankerous. Now, do what I told you."

"I don'—" Dondero suddenly decided the little man meant what he said, and getting shot, at least this early in the game, wasn't part of his brilliant scheme. He put the cuffs through the heavy handle of the door and with some maneuvering managed to click them about his wrists. The little man reached over with his free hand to check them, and then moved back, satisfied. He slid the gun onto a small tray built to the left of the steering wheel beneath the dash, and then leaned back, more relieved. Dondero stared at him.

"Okay, I'm cuffed. Now, what's all this? Who are you?"

"I said, a friend, didn't I? We got you out of the slammer, didn't we?"

"Slammer?"

135

"The clink, the jug. Jail," the little man said, and muttered, "Good God!" under his breath. He thought the dummy was supposed to speak English!

"Sure," Dondero said suspiciously. "For why?"

The little man looked at him with amusement. "You wouldn't kid me, would you, buster?"

"I don' understand."

"If you don't, buster, then you're even dumber than you look." His amused look turned into a grin. "And if you're as dumb as you sound, old George'll smarten you up. He's got a talent for that."

"What you mean? Who is dis ol' George?"

"I said, don't worry." The little man seemed to realize he was talking too much and lapsed into silence.

Dondero was just getting warmed up. "Why we sittin' here? We waitin' for somebody?"

"We ain't waiting for nobody. We're just waiting."

"Why?"

"Because I feel like waiting," the small man said shortly, and added almost grudgingly, "Anyway, it won't be for much longer."

There was a brief silence, then Dondero said, "Hungry."

He was proud of the conversational change of direction, although he had no notion as to what had suddenly made him say it. The fact was that at the moment he was sure he couldn't have eaten a thing, although a drink would certainly have been gratefully accepted. But he doubted the little man had a drink in the car, or would offer him one if he had it.

The little man frowned in his direction. "What?"

"Hungry. *Affamato*."

"What the hell—didn't they feed you in the joint?"

"Food *rifuiti*." Dondero made an expressive grimace. The little man didn't need to understand Italian to get the meaning.

"Well, I doubt we got much in the place, and we certainly ain't stopping at no McDonalds," the little man said, and looked at his wristwatch. He nodded; they were on schedule. "Okay, Pisano, we're on our way. It ought to be clear by now." He considered Dondero thoughtfully and then said, "Look, I'm going to blindfold you. Those are orders, so don't blame me. And don't try to butt me with your dome—guy did that to me once, almost bust my nose."

He picked an elastic ski band from the all-purpose tray beneath the dashboard and slipped it over Dondero's head, adjusting it so the wide portion covered the eyes. Satisfied with his handiwork, he slid back under the wheel, inserted the ignition key, and twisted it. A powerful and nearly silent motor sprang to life beneath them, rumbling quietly. The little man listened to it with evident pride for several moments, and then eased the car from its position beside the boxcar, swaying over the rough terrain until he bumped gently over a curb into a street. To Dondero's surprise they turned to the right, toward the bay, rather than to the left in the direction of Third Street; for a moment he wondered if they were to be picked up at some small dock and transported by water, after all, but the detour was only temporary, and then they turned again, heading north once more. One more turn and the car gathered speed as it crossed what Dondero judged to be Third Street in a rush, far from the bridge, and well north of Army. If Reardon was parked anywhere near the bridge, still wondering where Dondero had disappeared to, the blindfolded man thought, he was apt to wait there for a long time.

Beneath the lightly itching ski mask, Dondero tried to keep track of their location by counting dips at each intersection, trying to picture a map of the area in his mind and then place them upon it, as the car twisted and turned, but he soon gave it up. According to his calculations, they should have been halfway to Oakland, somewhere in the middle of the bay. In any event, he assumed he would know where they were when they stopped and the ski band was removed; in the meantime it was reassuring to think that if they had blindfolded him, they obviously had no immediate plans for killing him, since what difference would it make what he saw if he were going to end up in the bay in any case? On the other hand, he suddenly realized, the man they weren't planning on killing was an Italian fugitive named Patrone with some valuable answers, and not an upright, hard-working, well-intentioned—if overly nosey—cop, who could well be into something a trifle over his head.

The little man drove with the assured knowledge of both his

137

vehicle and the area. Dondero leaned his head against the cold glass, listening to the rhythmic clicking of the windshield wipers, and tried to blank his mind to whatever he would face when they arrived wherever they were going. Sufficient unto the day, or the night, he thought, and would have liked nothing better than to take a brief nap, but the constant braking and acceleration for the many corners made that impossible. He knew he should be thinking like mad, except he couldn't think of anything at the moment to think about. He bit back a yawn and waited.

They drove in this fashion for what Dondero judged to be approximately half an hour before he felt the car being braked. It halted, purring contentedly, and he heard the car door open and felt the car list slightly as the little man descended. There was a brief pause and then the screeching sound of a large motorized garage door being raised. Then the little man was back and they were driving inside a building. The motor revved once in a powerful roar; the garage door screeched its way to closing, and then there was silence. A small hand touched his wrist, one cuff was unlocked, and then relocked free of the hampering armrest. The small hand touched his forehead and the ski band was removed.

He looked up and saw a large man with a heavy beard studying him expressionlessly through the wet glass of the car window. Well, he thought, in for a nickel, in for a buck; he pushed down on the door handle with his handcuffed wrists, shoved the door open, and stepped from the car, raising himself to his full height, but the other man was still looking down on him from a much greater height.

"Hello, Patrone."

What attitude to take? Well, his mother always taught him that nobody ever got ahead in this world by being overly subservient, and even though any time he tried to disobey one of her orders he got himself a fat ear, it still struck him as being a basically proper teaching. He therefore paid no attention to the greeting but looked around coolly, noting that he was in what seemed to be the loading area of a factory of some sort. He tried to picture what part of the city was most apt to provide factory buildings, but dropped it as being highly unimportant. Instead he chose to bring his gaze back to the man facing him; he made his voice harsh.

"Okay, what in hell's all this about?"

If the little man who had driven the car noted any marked improvement in his captive's English, he made no mention of it, but remained beside the automobile, as if waiting. The big man with the beard smiled genially.

"Look, Patrone—Vito—we're not enemies; not really. We're on the same side, or we can be if you have any intelligence. You came over to this country to—but we can talk more comfortably upstairs."

Dondero masked his disappointment. Old hair-face might have waited until he got through saying exactly why Patrone had come to this country before he became so hospitable! He held a poker face, however, and followed the bearded man up a small flight of steps to the loading dock itself, and then along the platform to a freight elevator in one corner. The little man stayed behind with the car.

The elevator rose creakily in the silence and the gloom. Dondero wondered exactly what kind of place he was in; he knew it was a factory or a warehouse of some sort, but the nature of the operation was a mystery; the elevator doors effectively hid any sight of the floors they were passing. The cab stopped at the top floor and the two men got off. The bearded man opened a door set in a partition across a narrow corridor, and Dondero entered. He was not at all surprised to find that Pop Holland was not present. His analysis for all the reasons the kidnapper would keep the two apart, apparently, was sound. He looked about.

A comfortable sofa graced one wall of the large room, flanked on either side by small end tables. Colorful pictures were spaced tastefully on the walls, a wide desk occupied one corner of the room with a utility bar behind it; venetian blinds had been tilted as if to keep out light, but heavy closed shutters could be seen behind them at the edges.

The large man closed the door behind him, walked over and seated himself behind the desk, and waved a hand hospitably for Dondero to take a seat. Dondero managed to drag up an upholstered chair with his manacled hands and dropped into it. The bearded man lit a cigar, offered one to Dondero; Dondero shook his head and raised his manacles as if in explanation for his refusal. The bearded man appeared not to notice the gesture, but leaned back, puffing smoke, stroking his beard gently with his free hand.

"All right, Patrone—Vito—let's get down to business."

"I got no business with you," Dondero said, and tried to sound disdainful. He had no clue as to what he was talking about, but he did know he was at least stretching out an interview that could well end up uncomfortably for himself. He thought of Scheherazade and the thousand nights, and forced himself not to smile. "I got no business with anyone handles me like you handle me." He raised the manacles again.

The large man shrugged. "I'm afraid that's necessary for the moment. Certainly they are not uncomfortable; be patient and put up with them for the moment—"

"And I want dry clothes. I want—"

"Later," the bearded man said and leaned forward. "Let's forget what you want and get down to what I want. Where . . . ?"

"And another thing," Dondero said, frowning across the desk, "how much you have to pay to get me out of jail? And who you pay it to, huh? I meet a guy up there, good guy, maybe I buy him out, too."

The bearded man smiled. "I'm afraid we didn't buy you out of jail. I saw no necessity for wasting time determining the extent of corruption in our city police. No, we kidnapped a policeman and offered to trade him for you. It was that simple."

"What!" Dondero glared across the desk. "*Un vigile?* A cop? You kidnap him?" He shook his cuffed hands violently. "I got nothin' to do with no kidnap of a cop!"

George laughed, a small delightful laugh, somehow oddly out of place coming from the large body.

"Don't worry, my friend. As you say, you have nothing to do with the matter." The smiling face lost some of its jollity; the eyes studying Dondero turned cold. "The policeman need not concern you. You are here—"

"This *vigile*—you kill him?"

140

"I said, that scarcely concerns you—"

"What you say, it don' concern me!" Dondero glared at the bearded man and waved his hands excitedly, the manacles jangling. "Right now they got nothin' on me! Nothin'! I don' get mixed up in no kidnap, see? An' I don' get mixed up in no killin', either, see? They got nothin' on me, an' I don' get—"

"They have nothing on you?" The delightful laugh returned. "Oh, my dear friend! Please! They may not know what they have on you, but I do. So let's stop playing games—"

"I wan' a drink," Dondero suddenly said. He thought about it a moment and nodded. "Yeah, that's what I wan'. Hey, all I think about in the *figlio de madre carcere* is somethin' to drink, you know?"

George looked at him a moment, finally sighed, and swung his chair about. He searched the top of the small bar a moment, found a bottle that suited him, and poured a generous drink. He swung back, leaned over, and placed the glass on the far side of the desk.

"This is some of the finest cognac to ever come out of France. I hope you appreciate it."

Dondero showed his appreciation by clasping the glass in both hands, upending it, and taking the drink down in one gulp. He shuddered, grimaced, caught his breath, and then wiped his mouth on the back of one of his cuffed hands. He wiped that hand on his trouser leg and belched.

"Okay, I guess." He looked around the room and his eye fell on the sofa. "Hey, you know, the bed in that *figlio de madre carcere*, nobody can sleep on her. *Guanciale*, she's like stone." He suddenly yawned and came to his feet. "Hey, we talk in the morning, huh? Right now I think I sleep."

George's big hand slammed down on the desk in sudden fury; Dondero's empty glass jumped. Dondero looked down on the bearded man with a faint sneer.

"What's a matter?"

"Sit down."

The voice was dangerously quiet. Dondero shrugged and sat down again. "Okay, I sit. Now, what's a matter?"

"The matter," George said through his teeth, "is that we didn't get you out of jail just to watch you drink or watch you sleep. We—"

"Yeah," Dondero said, interested. "Why did you get me out of jail?"

"You know damn well! Where is the stuff?"

"Stuff?" Dondero looked puzzled. "I don' know what you talk about, you know?"

George took a deep breath and slowly exhaled it, managing to keep himself under control. He studied the insolent look on Dondero's face a moment and spoke quietly and clearly.

"Now, look, my friend. Listen and listen carefully. Before you continue with this charade about now knowing what I'm talking about, do you remember your friend Lazaretti?"

"Lazaretti ain' no friend of mine!"

"Lazaretti," George said slowly, "is no friend of anyone at the moment, unless it's the crabs on the bottom of the bay. You are probably not aware of it, but we first thought Lazaretti was the man we wanted, and last night we got our hands on him in what the police thought was a trade for their sergeant. In any event, before he died—and he died very poorly, my friend—he talked, or tried to talk. His English was practically nonexistent, and I had no intention of bringing anyone else into the deal just to serve as a translator. Still, he did make enough sense for us to gather that he was merely the bodyguard. You were the courier—"

Dondero wrinkled his forehead; it was not all acting. He looked like a man who was doing his best to understand someone speaking too rapidly in a language he didn't thoroughly understand. Still, he got the general idea. What he needed were details.

"Courier? What's a courier?"

"You still want to be cute, eh? A courier, my friend, is a man who carries things from one country to another. You brought the stuff in. You brought it in for someone else, it's true—and that someone else is just stupid enough to be waiting for you to get out of jail to take delivery—but I'm afraid it will be a little late for him by then."

Dondero maintained a poker face. Now, at least, the whole thing made sense. Although how knowing what it was all about

142

could help him at the moment was still one of the great mysteries. He brought his attention back to George and studied him through narrowed eyes.

"You think you know so much, maybe you don't know as much as you think you know."

George smiled. "No? You think I'm guessing? I don't go to this much trouble for guesses, my friend. You brought two and a half kilos of Turkish pure into this country a week ago. Let's stop playing games. I want to know where you hid it."

Dondero sneered. "An' if I don' tell you, then I gonna end up in the water with Lazaretti, huh?" He shook his head. "Then nobody ever goin' to find it, huh?"

The bearded man considered the tough unshaven face across from him for several moments, then took a deep breath.

"All right, Patrone. You can be broken, and if you think you can't, you're wrong. Your share in the deal is so damn small, anyway, that you'd crack the first time you started to hurt. But I'm getting tired of wasting time. So I won't even threaten you—I'll talk business with you."

Dondero nodded. "That's better. I don' like threats, you know?"

"And I don't like to make them. Let me put it this way—I know more about the deal than you think. You were paid the equivalent of five thousand dollars to bring the stuff in and deliver it. Five thousand lousy dollars!" He leaned forward, impressively. "If you'd even consider handing it over for that, you're a bloody fool. You've got a fortune there, man! Come in with me and we'll split right down the middle. I've got the best distribution system in the world, one that nobody can touch. Right here in this building I've got a system that makes all the rest of them look silly. No pushers, no street-corner exchanges in front of half the town, no kids selling in some dumb locker room. No chance, in short, of getting caught. Come on, Vito—come on in! It makes sense all around."

Dondero appeared to think about it. "Sure," he said at last. "It makes sense, but it only makes sense for you. I go for any deal like that, then the guy who hire me in Italy, he get mad, and I go down the street in Roma someday, and bang! bang!" Despite the manacles he managed to raise a pointed finger to his head, triggered by his thumb. "Then Vito Patrone, he's just a memory. Like Lazaretti." He shook his head dolorously. "I don' like it."

"Listen!" George said fiercely, scenting victory without the waste of time involved in torture, "don't be a bloody fool! You don't have to go back to Italy! You can be in Mexico tomorrow, or anywhere else you want to be! Hell, your share would be a kilo and a quarter of Turkish pure, and do you have any idea of what that's worth when I get through cutting it and spreading it around? Man, you can pick your spot—Hong Kong, Rio de Janeiro, Sydney—and live like a king!"

"Yeah, but—"

"But, what?"

"Hey, you know, them guys, they trusted me—"

George came as close to snorting as he ever permitted himself.

"Trusted you? Trusted you? Who do you think you're kidding? A man who made his living showing tourists the Trevi Fountain and the Spanish Steps, and then stole some loose change from their purses? Did you think I didn't know that? Trusted you? What do you think Lazaretti was doing traveling with you?" He waved that phase of the matter away as being of minor importance. "In any event, they wouldn't use you as a courier again, if you handed it over to them or not. Once is par for the course. I mean, they never use the same courier twice; why take the chance? So where does that leave you? Back to rolling little old ladies from Iowa for lunch money! Man, get smart!"

Dondero appeared to be thinking about it. "I don' know," he said at last, slowly. "I don' know. . . ." He looked around the room as if seeking some divine inspiration in arriving at so momentous a decision, and then spotted the sofa. He turned back to George, nodding his head. "I know. I sleep on it."

"Sleep on it, nothing! You'll tell me—"

Dondero's jaw hardened. "I sleep on it," he said simply.

George studied the tough face across from him a moment and then came to a decision, nodding. "All right, you sleep on it," he said. "You get a good night's rest and we'll talk about it in the morning."

"I sleep on it," Dondero said vaguely, and came to his feet, turning toward the comfortable-looking sofa. He suddenly seemed to realize he was still encumbered by the handcuffs. He raised them. "Hey, how about taking these off? I don' sleep so good with them on."

"We'll take them off when you've come to the proper decision," George said, and his faint smile was back. "And I'm afraid that sofa isn't as comfortable as it looks. Besides," he added, "there's nothing to handcuff you to there, you see. And I'm sure you can understand that we'd hate to lose you after all the trouble we had arranging your coming. No, we have a nice clean bedroom for you. . . ."

He reached into the top drawer of his desk, withdrew a revolver, checked it carefully, and came to his feet, gesturing toward the door.

"After you, please."

Dondero shrugged and shoved the door open to walk into the corridor. He hadn't exactly expected them to give him a car for a getaway, but he had gained a little time, at least, which he had a sad feeling he was going to waste actually sleeping. True, he had found out what the whole case was all about, but the question was, would he live long enough to pass the information along to the department? At the moment it looked doubtful. If he turned George's extremely generous offer down in the morning, he had a feeling George could turn nasty. And if he accepted it, how could he pretend to know where the stuff was stashed? It was a pretty problem.

Still, he was alive at the moment, which was a giant step in the right direction, and the bluff was working on all twelve cylinders. He wondered idly what decision he would have made if he really had two and a half kilos of Turkish pure hidden someplace. Probably go along with George's proposition, although it was highly doubtful that old George had much intention of allowing a confederate to live long enough to enjoy Lincoln Park, let alone Rio, or Hong Kong, or Sydney. It was what happened when you dealt with crooks; you couldn't trust them.

"Right here." George had stopped before a door. He opened it and stepped back for Dondero to enter. Dondero walked into the darkness and stood still while George reached in a hand and flipped on the light switch. Light flooded the room.

A gray-haired man was lying on one of the twin beds in the room. He looked up through feverish eyes. One hand was heavily and clumsily bandaged; his other was handcuffed to the bedstead.

"Hello, Don," he said weakly, and tried to sit up. "So you guys finally got here, huh . . . ?"

CHAPTER 12

Tuesday—9:00 A.M.

The rain had finally won the battle with the fog, and magnanimous in victory had swept off to the east, leaving the morning clear and cool. Lieutenant Reardon, pushing through the heavy glass doors of the Hall of Justice, glanced in the direction of the corner desk hoping for some message, received a negative shake of the head from the sergeant there, and continued on his way to the elevators. He walked into a waiting car, punched the button for the fourth floor, and rubbed his face wearily as the cab dutifully began its silent climb. He had slept not at all, lying in bed fully dressed, instead, waiting for the telephone to ring and to hear that sardonic voice, no longer smiling, inform him that their little ploy had failed, and that if they didn't stop fooling around and put the real Vito Patrone on the bridge at two the next morning, there would be two dead cops, and not one.

But there had been no call, and the elaborate equipment that had been hurriedly installed to trace any such call had apparently been wasted. Either Dondero was getting away with the bluff, at least for the time being, or the sardonic man had become a bit leery of a trap, which was not surprising. The kidnapper, whoever he was, was far from stupid; and he never seemed to contact the police with his messages twice at the same place.

The elevator stopped, the doors moved obediently back, and Reardon stared blankly out into the corridor, remembering where he was only when the doors began to close. He reached out in time to send them sliding back with a reproving hiss, and walked from the car shaking his head. Man, he thought, I'd better wake up before I step into an open manhole!

Stan Lundahl was shrugging himself into his jacket, happy that his extended graveyard shift was finally over, when Reardon walked into the office. Stan pulled his jacket straight, tugged his necktie into a semblance of respectability, and nodded.

"Hi, Lieutenant. How's it going?"

"Don't ask," Reardon said, and yawned deeply. He finished by stretching elaborately and considered Lundahl. "What's new around here? No meeting scheduled for this morning?"

"Not that I heard of. Nothing to meet about, I guess." Stan dug into a jacket pocket for cigarettes, pulled a pad of matches from his shirt pocket, and put the two of them together. "My guess is that the brass figure Pop is long gone, and more meetings won't bring him back. They'd just interfere with the work of getting the bastard who did it." He picked a shred of tobacco from his lip with a fingernail and looked at Reardon speculatively.

Reardon frowned. "What's the long look supposed to mean?"

"Nothing." Lundahl changed his look to one of curiosity. "Aren't you going to ask me about Dondero?"

Reardon woke up. "Oh. That's right. Anybody hear anything?"

Lundahl quit playing games. He had been waiting for the lieutenant to arrive in order to spring his news, and had just about given up when his superior had entered the office. He sank back into the chair behind his desk, prepared to spend a little bit more of his overtime.

"He had a boat, did you know that?" He went on before Reardon could perjure himself. "Yeah. A small fisherman he must have bought cheap and fixed up. Kept it down in Burlingame."

Reardon merely grunted. He walked over and sat down behind his desk.

"Yeah. Way we heard about it," Lundahl went on expansively, "the guy who sold it to him has a brother-in-law on the force. Patrol officer named Garrity, works out of Park Station. Anyway,

Garrity mentioned it to the guy when the two met about four this morning to go fishing, because the chief has cut out time-off until we get somewhere on this case, and Garrity was supposed to be off today, but instead he's got to be back on at nine, but he still wanted to get in some fishing . . ." He paused and frowned in a puzzled manner. "Can you imagine getting up at four o'clock in the morning just to catch a lousy fish?"

"Some guys do, I guess."

"Yeah. Anyway, this guy remembers about Dondero and the boat. Garrity called it in around five this morning. Said he hadn't been near a phone before. Probably waited until he caught his first swordfish, or whatever."

"And?"

"Well, anyway, it never occurred to this jughead Garrity that he was a police officer and maybe he should go down to Burlingame to check it out—hell no, he had to go fishing!" Lundahl shook his head at the idiocy of some people. "So, anyway, it filtered down to me a little after six this morning. Nobody else around, so I took a drive down there. Just got back, matter of fact."

Reardon tried to sound curious. "What did you find?"

"Well"—Lundahl paused to light a fresh cigarette from the old butt before continuing—"somebody's been using the boat mighty recently, and it stands to reason it was Don. He wasn't there, but he had to hang out someplace, didn't he?"

"I guess."

"Yeah, And the hatchway was locked with a padlock, and no sign of any break-in," Lundahl went on, "that is, until I pried the hasp off to get in, of course. It's his boat, all right—owner's certificate in the cabin, framed on the wall, fishing license tucked in the corner of the frame. Anyway, to get back to this morning, there were wet footprints on the hatchway steps, and the same wet prints down in the cabin. They had to be from last night because it hasn't rained in a week, and they would have dried up by now if they were old ones, don't you think?"

"I think," Reardon said, his face expressionless. "Go ahead. You're doing fine."

"Yeah," Lundahl said, and leaned over to flick ashes toward the wastebasket. He leaned back and continued with his story. "Matter of fact, there were two sets of footprints; the ones from the wet shoe, like on the steps, and some sneaker prints on top of them in a couple places, and also on the linoleum of the cabin floor. The sneakers were there over to one side, like they were kicked off, you know. They had Don's name inside them marked in ink."

"Maybe he made both the prints," Reardon suggested. "Maybe he changed shoes before he went out. He may have come back for something—a raincoat, maybe—and managed to make both sets of prints. After all, nobody would go out in sneakers on a night like last night, not if he had anything else to wear."

"No, sir." Lundahl shook his head. "The sneakers and the shoes were different sizes. There was a pair of dungarees on the floor, too, like he changed clothes. Also, funny thing—there was his raincoat there, hanging up on a hook. Not that he couldn't have two raincoats, of course, but this one was the one he always wears around here. And another thing that makes me sure somebody else was there last night; there were two glasses out for liquor. Only one had been used, but the glasses were regularly kept in a little cabinet in swivel holders, so they wouldn't slide and break, and somebody had taken out two glasses and left them where they could have fallen and broken. Just a miracle they didn't. No, my guess is that Don was holing up in his boat, and last night after it started to rain he had a visitor, and for some reason or other he went off with the guy, leaving his raincoat behind. I know it sounds crazy, but that's the way I read it."

One of these days, Reardon thought, Stan Lundahl will be getting a promotion, if he isn't careful. He considered the other man steadily as he thought of a proper response.

"He went out without a raincoat in that weather last night?"

"I know." Lundahl shrugged. "Every time I've seen him with a raincoat it was the one I saw on the boat, so I figure it was the only one he had. I've only got one."

"But why would he do it?"

"He must have had a good reason," Lundahl said cheerfully, and crushed out his cigarette. "No sign of violence in the cabin. He just changed clothes and went off with this guy."

"In whose car?"

"The other guy's," Lundahl said. "Don's car's still in the garage at his apartment. I figure he went out to the boat by bus, or something, hung around there until this other man came. It had to be after midnight, because that's when it really started to rain. Washed away any tracks of the car, but that's how they had to leave. The last bus that passes that part of the road in Burlingame passes at midnight, sharp."

Reardon nodded. Lundahl had done a good job. "Anything else?"

"Yeah," Lundahl said slowly. "Those glasses that were out for drinks; I handled them real carefully. In the light you could see there were fingerprints on the two glasses, and even without equipment you could see they were different."

Reardon looked at Lundahl speculatively. "Fingerprints, eh?"

"Yes, sir."

"Did you bring them in?"

"Of course," Lundahl said. "They're in the side drawer of your desk."

Reardon frowned in surprise. "My desk? Why didn't you take them down to the lab?"

"Lieutenant," Lundahl said quietly, "if I'm wrong, all you have to do is send those glasses down to the lab yourself. But if I'm right, then you knew all about that boat of Don's, because he tells you about everything; and you were out there last night and you and Don have something cooking between the two of you, and if you wanted me to know what it was, you'd tell me." He looked Reardon in the eye. "Right?"

Reardon's expression didn't change in the least. "You're telling the story."

Lundahl shook another cigarette free, considered it a moment, and then shoved it back into the pack. "I'm smoking too much," he said, and came to his feet. He considered his superior a moment. "I'm all through telling any stories, Lieutenant. I've been on duty a long time, and I'm going home to get some rest." He raised a hand. "Have a good day, Lieutenant."

Reardon watched the tall angular man walk from the room. He sighed. Here was Dondero off on a wild-eyed scheme he should have been stopped from touching with a ten-foot pole; and now Lundahl was joining the club. Department rules were taking a beating, and those rules had been promulgated for good and sufficient reasons. Nor was it even faintly possible that any discipline committee would ever accept good intentions as an excuse for violating all the sacred precepts of the department. Even worse, it was very doubtful that the flaunting of the rules would get them one step closer to Pop Holland's kidnapper. In fact, they had probably made things worse by letting Dondero have his head.

Still, he had to admit with a touch of pride in his group, Lundahl had done a very nice bit of thinking on the job, and should have been complimented. And then had his head handed to him for not having put his suspicions on paper and seen that they were distributed throughout the Hall. . . !

CHAPTER 13

Tuesday—9:35 A.M.

Foot Patrolman Daniel C. Gottlieb reached his call box in ample time for this, his first report of the day, prepared as always to advise his sergeant that nothing of earth-shaking importance had occurred between the time he had left his home station in the Mission District and the time he had arrived on his beat. Then he paused in surprise, for it appeared that something had happened after all, albeit not very much. It seemed someone had gone to the trouble of prying open the door of the call box, and the only reason for going to this much bother had to be mischief, since the little telephone inside was of no inherent value, and could only be used to speak either with the Mission Police Station or the Communications Center at the Hall of Justice. It didn't even have a dial to permit other calls. In addition, he noted that whoever had pried the door open had gone to the additional labor of refastening the door with a bit of cord, as if to make sure the door did not bang in the wind and possibly disturb someone, although this consideration was largely wasted, since the neighborhood where Patrolman Gottlieb's call box was located was quite deserted.

Patrolman Gottlieb unwound the cord with a slight touch of excitement. His beat in this quiet section of the sprawling city usually produced little activity worthy of revelation to his superiors, and now, at least, he could begin the new day with a report of vandalism, even though the purpose of the vandal had been no more than the mere breaking of a patrolman's box. Still, it was city property, or county property—Patrolman Gottlieb wasn't sure which—which all citizens were importuned to respect, and he opened the box prepared to transmit all vital details to the desk sergeant at Mission. But then he paused, frowning, for it appeared that whoever had vandalized the call box had not done so without a purpose. They had apparently done so in order to leave behind a sealed envelope tucked between the old-fashioned mouthpiece and the back wall of the metal box. Patrolman Gottlieb removed the envelope and studied it closely.

It was addressed to one Lieutenant James Reardon, and Patrolman Gottlieb knew very well that Lieutenant James Reardon was one of the brighter lights in the Homicide Division, and that the message was undoubtedly meant for him and not for any Lieutenant Reardon in the Army, or the Navy, or even the Fire Department, although they also boasted lieutenants, a fair share of whom were probably named Reardon. Besides, if the note were intended for someone in the Fire Department, why hadn't it been left in a fire box, of which there were even more in the city than patrolmen's call boxes?

No, the note was clearly meant for Lieutenant James Reardon of Homicide, and Patrolman Gottlieb had a strong feeling it was important that the lieutenant receive the message as soon as possible. For, among other things, such as the method of delivery, there was something quite mysterious in the manner the vandal had addressed the envelope, what with each letter apparently of a different size and cut from some magazine or newspaper and pasted in place. Patrolman Gottlieb knew this to be suspicious in the extreme, clearly indicating someone's desire to avoid self-identification.

Convinced that this was only the first step on the sure path to promotion, and subconsciously thanking the vandal for having chosen this particular call box for the leaving of the envelope, Patrolman Gottlieb raised the receiver and pressed the button connecting him to the Hall of Justice, asking that a patrol car be sent around at once to pick the message up and deliver it. He only refrained with effort from adding that Gottlieb was spelled with two "t"s.

Tuesday—9:45 A.M.

One of the many things that often puzzled Lieutenant Reardon was how his lovely Jan could possibly consider his work dangerous, when 95 per cent of his working day seemed to be spent either in putting words on paper or in attempting to make some sense from papers upon which others had spent hours putting words. If they gave service awards for writer's cramp, he often thought, or for strained eyesight, a man could retire from the police force after five years with a chest full of medals that would have made a five-star general jealous.

The ringing of the telephone spared him from one more report. He gladly put it aside and picked up the receiver, grunting into it.

"Reardon, here."

"Hello, Jim? Roy Gentry. How'd you like to get a preview of a report that's about to go up to the chief?"

"Why a preview?"

"Because the chief is out of the Hall at the moment, and Homicide will be getting a copy anyway after the chief sees it, and I thought maybe you wouldn't want to wait."

And you also have found something you feel you can brag about, Reardon thought; and I hope you're right. I'll be the first to kiss you on both cheeks.

"I'll be right there," he said, and happily shoved papers aside, coming to his feet. His departure was delayed, however, by a repeat of the telephone ring. Reardon sighed and picked it up.

"Reardon, here."

"Sergeant Martin, Communications, Lieutenant. We just received a call from one of the foot patrolmen out of Mission. He was checking in at his box and found it broken open. Somebody had left a sealed envelope inside, tucked between the mouthpiece and the wall. It was addressed to you."

155

Reardon leaned back against his desk, taking some of the weight off his feet. His eyes were narrowed. "What did it say?"

"He didn't open it," the sergeant said. "Like I said, it was sealed. He asked for a patrol car to pick it up and take it down to the Hall for you. We sent the nearest car we had. It ought to be there and back in a couple more minutes."

"Very gentlemanly not to open other people's mail," Reardon murmured.

"Sir?"

"Nothing. I'll be down in the lab with Roy Gentry when it gets here."

"Right, sir."

Reardon hung up the telephone and stared at it a moment in thought, an uncomfortable feeling in the pit of his stomach. He knew he had been expecting a message from the kidnapper ever since Dondero had disappeared from that bridge that night before, and he wished that knuckle-headed patrolman had had the sense to open the envelope and relay the message. And the kidnapper, whoever he was, remained as cagey as ever. Using the call box would assure him relatively quick delivery—quicker than the post office, surely—and be almost impossible to trace.

Because in Reardon's mind there was no doubt the message was from the kidnapper. Well, the bastard was still keeping his distance ahead of them all, but he had to slip sometime. They all did, sooner or later, according to the book; although nothing in the book had told him to put Dondero in jeopardy tgether with Pop. He sighed, hitched himself from the desk, and headed for the door.

He trotted down the steps to the floor below, walked down the corridor to the end, and pushed through the swinging doors to the laboratory. He nodded to the people working at the various benches and continued on through two more sterile-looking rooms to the small private laboratory Roy Gentry usually used to verify results obtained by subordinates in other sections of his department. Gentry was bending over a microscope, his horn-rimmed glasses perched on his head out of the way, while his ever-present cigarette was held as far from his work as possible, as if to avoid

156

contamination of his samples. Reardon came up behind him, plucked the cigarette from the extended fingers, and placed it neatly in an ashtray. Gentry looked up.

"Oh. Hi, Jim. Want to take a look?"

"Sure, but where's the report?"

Gentry pulled his glasses into place, tucked his cigarette back into one corner of his mouth, and jerked a thumb toward the small office in one corner of the room.

"On my desk," he said, speaking around smoke. "But this is all part of it. Thought you might be interested."

So let him show off, Reardon thought. I just hope it's worth bragging about. He bent over the microscope and adjusted the knob to bring the surface of the slide into focus. In his circle of vision, coming from blur to sharp image, was what seemed to be, in principal, a grayish stain with a series of darker streaks throughout. Reardon changed lenses, bringing up the magnification, since he knew he couldn't read as much into these mysteries as Roy Gentry.

Now the streaks seemed to have little various colored nodules attached to them, and were in turn attached to each other by little stems. Lighter bluish-colored random shapes were scattered throughout the area of vision, almost as if added as an afterthought. It looks like a moonscape, Reardon thought, and straightened up.

"It's beautiful," he said. "What is it?"

"Dark air-cured." Gentry was smiling proudly.

"Dark air-cured what?"

"Tobacco," Gentry said, not at all surprised by the other's ignorance. "Tobacco ash, that is."

"And what's so impressive about that?" He looked at the cigarette in Gentry's hand and nodded. "I see. You're checking the stuff you're smoking these days. You're trying to figure out if you can't come up with something cheaper, using old broom straws or something."

"No," Gentry said, not at all disturbed by this Philistinism. "That, my friend, came from the stuff collected from the floor of the back seat of Mike Holland's Chevy by Frank Wilkins and his crew. It was found on the portion of the back seat behind the passenger side of the car. It indicates that whoever was sitting in the back seat was smoking—"

Reardon stared at him a moment and then broke into a grin.

"For this you need a microscope? My old mother, bless her soul, never smoked a day in her life, but she sure as the devil saw enough cigarette ash on my father's jacket lapels! She could have saved you scientific geniuses a lot of work. Good grief! A microscope to tell tobacco ash! And as far as it being on the floor of the car in the back," he added, playing the devil's advocate, "it was probably from someone Pop gave a lift to fourteen years ago when the car was new, or maybe even a neighbor he took to the ball game last week."

"No," Gentry said evenly. He was enjoying himself. "A guest doesn't usually drop ashes on the floor, not in those quantities; he uses the ashtrays. And the ashtrays were clean, unused. The rest of the car was clean, too, so we can assume Mike kept it that way normally. Therefore, finding ash where it was found clearly indicates to me that the man who dropped that ash dropped it quite recently, and most probably was the man who kidnapped Mike Holland."

Reardon considered the idea and shook his head. "That still doesn't sound too conclusive to me. Mike may not have cleaned the car for weeks—"

"No," Gentry said calmly. Behind his thick glasses his eyes were twinkling. "You'll also note—if you can note the difference —that there is very little black dust mixed with the ash, and in this town, as in most towns unfortunately these days, it doesn't take very long for dust to settle."

"In a car with the windows closed?"

"Even in a car with the windows closed; modern cars certainly aren't dustproof. And we don't know they were always closed. We just know when the car was found, all the windows were closed, except the one across from the driver, which was partially open."

"All right," Reardon said, happy to agree. "Let's assume that the man who kidnapped Pop smoked. So what? Half the idiotic population of the entire country smokes—present company included."

"Actually, less than twenty-five per cent," Gentry said, ever the pedantic, "although that statistic includes children, of course, too young to smoke." He puffed on his cigarette with enjoyment as he went on. "However, the percentage is smaller for those who smoke cigars."

Reardon frowned. "Cigars?"

"That's right." Gentry was enjoying his triumph. "The ash is definitely from a cigar."

"Look," Reardon said, "I know you can tell a lot from tobacco ash in the laboratory, but it still seems a little Sherlock Holmes-ish, again, to me. So tell me, Holmes, how do you deduce the ash was from a cigar? And don't tell me you found the cigar band on the floor of the back seat."

Gentry shook his head unhappily.

"I wish we had. You see, we can't go as far as Holmes. He was supposed to be able to identify every known make of cigar and tobacco by its ash, but we're satisfied to be able to distinguish between the eight basic classifications of tobacco by their ash—flue-cured, dark air-cured, oriental and semi-oriental, dark sun-cured, Burley—"

"All right! All right! I believe you. So?"

"So each type leaves a distinctive ash." Gentry gestured toward the microscope. "That is dark air-cured, which is used almost exclusively for cigars. Unless," he added with dry humor, "the man was smoking a hookah in the back seat, because dark air-cured is also used in water pipes in the Middle East. But of course," he said, thinking about it, "there wouldn't have been any ash at all with a hookah, would there?"

"I doubt it. Look, Roy—"

"Now, cigarettes, of course, are blends, either of whatever the smoker prefers, or what is available at a good price, or whatever the manufacturer feels like putting in at the moment," Gentry went on, now wound up. He smiled. "Sherlock Holmes would have gone crazy in today's cigarette market." His smile disappeared; the lecturer returned. "Most American cigarettes contain a blend of flue-cured, oriental, and Burley, with or without Maryland light air-cured. English cigarettes are wholly flue-cured tobacco with no additives permitted by law, other than water. Pipe tobaccos—"

Reardon interrupted at last, weary of more knowledge.

"Look, Roy, I'll read about it in your report, if you don't mind."

"If you wish." Gentry was not at all disturbed; his show was scarcely half over. He turned to a second microscope. "Now, here we have an example of hair. You might know that the man was bearded—"

Reardon was quite aware of the magic sometimes developed in a police laboratory, and he knew that hair gave many more clues than most people knew. Still, it seemed a pity to break up Gentry's triumphant mood.

"All right, Roy, I'll play the straight man. How do you know he was bearded?"

Gentry crushed out his cigarette and automatically reached for another.

"When we first separated the stuff Frank Wilkins vacuumed from various parts of the car, we found among the vacuum cleanings of the back seat, in addition to ash, hair. Now, hair," he said, thinking about it, "is of great importance in identification. Not only can race and sex be determined by microscopic evaluation of hair, but even age can be roughly calculated. Not to the year, of course, but childhood can be differentiated from youth, youth from middle age, middle age from old age, and so forth. In addition, hair from different parts of the body varies considerably in appearance under a microscope. According to Belfield, the hair of the male beard is readily distinguishable from scalp hair by diameter, shape, and pigmentation. The hairs of the scalp generally vary from $\frac{1}{200}$ to $\frac{1}{1000}$ of an inch in diameter, while the hairs from the jaw are larger, varying in diameter from about $\frac{1}{150}$ to—"

"All right!" Reardon modified his tone. "All right, Roy. Do you mind? I appreciate the job you've done, but give it to me in nice short sentences. What race, sex, and age are we talking about?"

160

Gentry nodded, pleased with the reaction of the other man. He brought his exposition to a properly dramatic close.

"The man we're talking about—the man I am assuming kidnapped Pop Holland—is a white male, between twenty-five and forty years of age, with a beard at least three inches in length and possibly more, beginning to gray at the tips, who smokes cigars. As you know from our voice graphs, we assume him to be a native Californian, probably raised in the bay area, and with a decent education, no doubt at least some college."

"And a nasty habit of hurting people," Reardon added. "Also accompanied by a small companion who isn't any angel himself, considering we figure he was driving the car when the wino was run over."

He drummed his fingers on the laboratory bench absently while he went over it all in his mind. There were undoubtedly many hundreds of people who fit the physical appearance that Gentry had magically evoked from his microscope and his voice comparator, but the lieutenant had to admit they were a lot farther along than they had been, and a lot farther along than he had expected to be. Still it was a long way from being sufficiently identitive to permit the issuance of an all-points bulletin. If only they could pinpoint the kidnapper a bit more accurately; if only they had one or two more descriptive elements to narrow the field! Well, maybe the message that had been left in the patrolman's call box might give them what they lacked, though it was doubtful if the kidnapper would make that hoped-for mistake.

As if in answer to the thought, the door swung back and one of the uniformed officers from the reception desk in the lobby was there, holding out a crumpled envelope.

"Not much chance for fingerprints," he said apologetically. "The patrol car driver said the footman who gave him this was hanging onto it like it was his birthday present. Ruined any possibility of prints." He added under his breath, "The dummy!"

"Don't worry about it," Reardon said shortly. "This guy doesn't leave prints." He studied the pasted letters on the envelope a moment, and then slipped a finger under the flap, ripping open the cover. He removed the single sheet of paper, unfolded it, and read it. The words, also clipped from a newspaper or magazine, were of varying sizes and type shapes, but together they formed a message that was short and to the point:

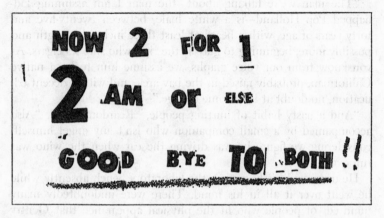

The words were evidently cut from the same newspaper or leaflet as the letters on the envelope; and the underlining of the last four words, as well as the exclamation points, had been added using a heavy black marking pencil. Reardon read it again, although the message was clear enough. He felt a sickening feeling in his stomach. He should never have permitted Dondero to go ahead with his harebrained scheme! Permitted? He practically abetted it! Which was what came from desperation and frustration. Idiot! He forced down the fury he felt at himself and handed the note and envelope both to the laboratory head.

"Okay, Roy," he said heavily. "This is the only tangible thing we have from the man, other than that first tape. What can you dig out of this to add to what we've got? And maybe give us enough to nail the bastard!"

Gentry took the paper and envelope. He looked at the envelope briefly and then concentrated on the note. He looked up, curious.

"What does he mean, *two* for one? And 'good bye to *both*'?"

"Never mind," Reardon said shortly. "Forget the words—concentrate on the note itself. Give me something to work on."

Gentry studied the angry face a moment and then shrugged. He considered the sheet once again, and then placed it on the bench; his glasses went back up to his forehead and he bent over the paper, studying it through a large lens he took from the jacket pocket of his laboratory coat. Reardon waited impatiently while the tall thin man scanned the letters carefully. Gentry looked at the pencil markings last and then looked up. He sounded and looked apologetic.

"Printing isn't our big forte, but I can make some educated guesses. Obviously, none of these letters came from any magazine, but rather from newsprint stock of some sort. Secondly, I'd say the paper the letters were printed on was the same grade paper stock as the paper the words were pasted on, which is a bit unusual—"

"Unusual? In what way?"

"Well, now." Gentry said logically, "if you were cutting out letters to paste up a message, from the evening newspaper, for example, what would you normally paste them on?"

Reardon stared at him a moment in dawning understanding and then nodded.

"I see! You'd scarcely have some of the same blank newsprint around the house, would you?" Could his bearded, cigar-smoking, sardonic adversary finally have made a mistake? If so, it was a dandy! Reardon picked up the note, folded it along the original creases carefully, and replaced it in the envelope.

Gentry frowned. "Don't you want us to work on that?"

"You keep working on what you have," Reardon said, and tucked the envelope into his pocket.

"And what are you going to go?"

"Something I should have done long ago," Reardon said grimly. "Do some work myself!"

CHAPTER 14

Lieutenant Reardon parked his Charger on Mason, around the corner from the new, impressive four-story building that contained the San Francisco *Express*. As the first new newspaper in the city since the demise of the old *Call-Bulletin*, it was rumored that the *Express* was having its problems combatting the age-old prestige of the *Chronicle* and the sheer power of the *Examiner*. Still, Reardon wished the newcomer all the luck in the world—especially if it could provide him answers to some questions. There was, of course, the ridiculous question Porky Frank thought he should ask, as to who might have known about the dinner arrangements for Pop Holland's retirement party; and then there were the far more important questions arising from the pasted-up note Reardon was guarding in his jacket pocket.

He trotted up the two steps to the wide glass doors, pushed through into a lobby dominated by a huge globe of the world rotating slowly overhead, and advanced to the information desk beneath the round monstrosity. The only person he even had the slightest contact with was whoever wrote the "View from Nob Hill" column, so he felt he might as well start with him. He nodded to the girl behind the desk pleasantly.

"Miss?"

She smiled up. "Sir?"

"I'd like to see—"

Reardon suddenly paused, a tingle passing through him. Ever since he had entered the building he had subconsciously been aware of a faint throbbing somewhere in the background; but now the sound intruded upon him consciously, like the incipient rumblings of an approaching earthquake, except that now he was so immediately aware of it, there was a certain definite rhythm to the sound. He could feel the slight beat that accompanied the sound coming through the marble-tiled floor to the soles of his feet. He didn't need to listen to it very long. It was a sound that was engraved upon his memory for all time. He swung back to the girl, his pleasant expression gone.

"What's that noise? That rumbling?"

The girl smiled indulgently. "Everybody asks that. It's not the San Andreas fault, though I guess that's what most people think, the first time they come here. It's just our presses rolling, sir. I'm so used to them I don't even hear them any more." That quite-normal inquiry satisfied, the girl smiled brightly. "Now, can I help you, sir?"

But Reardon wasn't listening. His mind was racing. Newspaper presses, eh? That tape had been made in a building with newspaper presses, and the man who made it was probably like the receptionist—he was so used to the sound he hadn't even realized it was there, providing a clue to the police. And the note that had arrived that morning, containing the pasted-up threat; that note had been cut from a newspaper and pasted up on blank newsprint, and where was the easiest place to have newsprint lying around if not at a newspaper plant? And then there had been a columnist—one who chose not to sign his name—who was quite openly disdainful of the police. . . .

The entire series of connecting ideas swept across the lieutenant's brain in analytical process, completed in seconds. He stared at the girl.

"Miss, who writes the column 'View from Nob Hill'?"

The smile remained, but now it was frozen, no longer as friendly as before, but maintained because that was one of the requirements of meeting the public.

"I'm afraid we're not allowed to give out that information, sir."

Reardon's jaw tightened. A conspiracy, eh? He reached into his pocket, extracting his billfold, opening it to expose his warrant card on one side and his lieutenant's shield on the other. He allowed the girl to study it a moment, and then closed it and restored it to his pocket. His voice became official.

"All right, miss. My name is Lieutenant Reardon, and I asked you a question! Who writes that column? And why doesn't it carry his name, as every other column in the paper does?"

The girl looked startled by the attack. "I—I'll have to make a call, sir."

Reardon reached over the desk, clamping his hand tightly on the phone.

"No calls! Who writes that column? And why the big secret?"

The girl looked terrified. Tears began to well in her eyes.

"I can't—"

"Then we'll take a trip down to the Hall of Justice and see if we can't get some information out of you down there!" Reardon said grimly. "Let's go!"

"No! I—" The tears came in a flood. The girl looked miserable. "I'll tell you. It's—it's Mr. Maxwell. He's the publisher. He—"

She looked around as if for help, but the lobby remained empty except for the two of them. Her teary eyes came back to Reardon's hard face.

"It's—he doesn't sign the column because he often, in fact most of the time, writes editorials in direct contradiction of his column. It's just—he says he does it to generate interest. Nobody outside the paper is supposed to know. . . ."

Reardon released the telephone, but stayed close enough to take charge if the girl tried to call for help. Maxwell, eh? And a devious man, too! Add that to the pot!

"Is this Maxwell in the building?"

"No. He—he hasn't come in, yet."

Just one more thing and we'll have it all tied up! Reardon thought. "And tell me this—does Mr. Maxwell happen to have a beard? And does he smoke cigars?"

There was the sound of the twin glass doors being opened before the girl could answer; Reardon turned to find a small,

166

portly white-haired gentleman dressed in extremely mod clothes for one his age come bustling up to the desk. He looked like Charlie Winninger to Reardon's eyes, and he wished the little man had waited a moment longer before breaking into his interview. The newcomer beamed at the girl.

"Ah, Jane! Good morning! How's everything this morning?" The little beaming man seemed to notice for the first time that the girl had been crying. He glanced at Reardon sharply, as if to determine if this man might be the cause of the girl's unhappiness, and then brought his attention back to the receptionist. "Is something the matter?"

It was too much for the girl. She burst into tears again. "Oh, Mr. Maxwell . . . !"

Maxwell frowned and turned to Reardon. "What on earth seems to be bothering the girl? Did you do something, or say something?"

Reardon felt his face getting red. His theory disintegrated about him. He brought out his billfold for the second time and opened it for Mr. Maxwell's inspection. Maxwell looked puzzled.

"Are you going to arrest her? On what grounds? I'm afraid we'll have to have our company attorneys look into this. I've known Jane since she was a child. Her father—"

"No, no!" Reardon said hurriedly, and felt foolish. "It has nothing to do with the girl. It's—well, sir, I was asking her questions about you."

"About me?" Maxwell's deep blue eyes considered Reardon sharply. "I see. Well, the one to properly ask questions about me would be me, don't you think? Come along." He turned and trotted off about the back of the reception desk in the direction of the elevators, calling back over his shoulder, "It's all right, Jane. It's all right. . . ."

Reardon followed the small man into the elevator. They rose in silence to the top floor, and emerged into a room filled with desks and people and noise; the steady ringing of telephones drowned out the strange rhythmic sound of the presses downstairs, but the faint bumping could still be felt through the floor. Maxwell pressed through the crowded room without paying the slightest attention to the racket about him, nor did anyone bother to look up or greet him as the small man and Reardon passed. They reached a corner office and Maxwell courteously held the door open until his guest had entered; he then followed along, leaving a small hissing cylinder to shut the door, and trotted to his desk, seating himself and gesturing toward a chair, all in the same motion. He smiled at his guest and pressed a button on his intercommunicator.

"Miss Tenefly? No calls, no interruptions. I'll be in conference until further notice." He clicked the button upward and leaned back in his chair, fixing Reardon with a shrewd look. "All right, Lieutenant. Suppose you tell me what this is all about." A sudden thought came to him and he leaned forward, frowning. "Reardon! Lieutenant Reardon! Good God, I hope it had nothing to do with that column about the police! But I wrote an editorial the same day—" He stopped abruptly. "I mean—"

Reardon smiled. "The girl downstairs told me. I'll keep it a secret." His smile disappeared. "No, it has nothing to do with that column. Or it does, actually, in a way. . . ."

And it did, in a way, he thought, because if Porky Frank hadn't kept harping on that column, he didn't know whether he would have been here or not. He stared at the round little man a moment and then pulled up a chair and sat down across the desk from him. He watched the steady shrewd blue eyes a moment and made up his mind. After all, you had to trust somebody in this world, and if you couldn't trust the Charlie Winninger types, who could you trust? He wasn't sure that Captain Tower or Chief Boynton would have agreed with him, but the fact was that time was rapidly running out. He took a deep breath.

"Mr. Maxwell, I need help. That's why I came here this morning, but when I got here I got sidetracked with a stupid idea, and that's how I came to upset your receptionist. I think I'm back on the track now. I've got a story to tell you, but first I want to tell you—not ask you—that it cannot be published without our permission. Is that understood?"

Maxwell nodded. "Understood. Provided when permission is granted, the *Express* gets first crack."

"If you prove helpful," Reardon said flatly, and went on. "I'll put it very briefly. Four days ago we had a police officer kidnapped, and last night another one was taken. The kidnapper was very insistent that no publicity be given, which is why you have not heard of this before, although we would have held back on publicity regardless of his instructions. That's also why I asked you not to publish anything of what I am telling you, without permission."

He paused to put his thoughts in order and then continued.

"Now, whoever is holding these two officers has offered to release them in exchange for certain men in our custody. The crimes for which the men in our custody are being held are very minor, and I doubt if you would recognize their names if you heard them." He paused, thinking. "Or maybe you would. Guillermo Lazaretti and Vito Patrone."

Maxwell shook his head. "The names ring no bells."

"I didn't expect them to. However, I may ask you later to see if possibly one of your stringers turned in a story about their arrest, but at the moment it's not too important. At any rate the decision was made by the Hall of Justice not to accede to what amounted to blackmail demands on the part of kidnappers; the feeling was that if we began trading kidnapped officers for criminals in custody, no officer would be safe in the future."

"I agree," Maxwell said bluntly.

"I suppose I do, too. In any event, we received several messages from the kidnapper, the first one being on tape. We also recovered the automobile in which the first officer was kidnapped. The details of how our laboratory got their results are unimportant, but I can say that we were able to determine that the kidnapper is a fairly well-educated man who we believe was raised in the bay area and who is bearded and smokes cigars. He is accompanied by an accomplice who drove the kidnap car, who we believe is about five-foot-four inches tall."

Maxwell smiled bleakly. "About my size."

"I'd put you at closer to five-foot-six," Reardon said, and smiled mischievously. "However, just for fun, where were you last Saturday morning between nine and ten o'clock?"

Maxwell was not at all disturbed by the inquiry. He swung around in his swivel chair and reached for his desk diary, flipping it open. He leafed through a few pages and paused.

"Saturday, September fourth," he said. "At that hour I was having breakfast at the Peninsula Golf Club with the mayor, prior to a round of golf." He closed the book and swiveled back. "Our waiter was Tom. I had shirred eggs and a sweet roll. Now, you were saying?"

Reardon started to smile and then wiped it away.

"Does the description I just gave you ring any particular bell?"

Maxwell shook his head. "I'm afraid it also rings no bell."

Reardon sighed and plowed on, wondering if he was wasting his time. "I mentioned Saturday because at that hour the smaller accomplice was killing someone up in Potrero. However, to get back to the story—we also have evidence that indicates the kidnapper taped his message to us in a building where printing presses were in operation."

Maxwell tented his fingers and watched Reardon thoughtfully over them. He almost seemed to be composing the first line of either his column or an editorial, probably, Reardon thought, on the dangers in the street or the idiocy of the police. He went on:

"Then this morning we received a second message. This one was made up of letters and words cut out of what seems to be a newspaper, pasted on a sheet of paper. Our laboratory believes the letters were all cut from the same paper. And they think the paper the words were pasted on was the same paper as the letters and words were printed on." He reached into his pocket and brought out the envelope, handling it gingerly. He eased the note from the envelope, unfolded it, and laid it on the desk. Maxwell leaned over and studied it closely. His nose wrinkled at the message.

"I assume the 2 A.M. is tomorrow morning?"

"Yes."

"Hmmm." Maxwell leaned back in his chair, studying the sheet from a distance, and then sat erect. "You know, Lieutenant," he said slowly, "newspapers also operate in the manner of a detective bureau at times. Take those two lads from the Washington *Post*, in the Watergate case. They certainly did a better job than the police in that city; or than the FBI, for that matter, even assuming the bureau was trying." He pointed toward the note. "Now, I think it's quite possible one or two of our old compositors might be able to read more into this note than the police can—or than I can, frankly. I'll need your permission to call one of them in and ask him." He paused. "Or maybe you'd feel better if I cut the message into separate words and moved them around to change the meaning?"

Reardon sat up. "No! You can have one of your people look at it—in fact I'd appreciate it—but let's leave the note intact. It may well be evidence in a murder trial someday."

"Of course." Maxwell shrugged. "Oh, well, if I know the man I want to show this to, he won't even read it. He'll just look at the type and the paper." He leaned over and flipped the communicator switch. "Miss Tenefly? Get McDougal up here, will you? On the double." He clicked off the set and leaned back. "Well, let's see what the Scots Wizard has to say."

They waited in silence, Maxwell tapping his tented fingers together, Reardon staring from the window, wondering if he was right in being here at all. There really had been no need to give Maxwell the information he had; all that any other police officer would have done would have been to show his shield and ask the questions he wanted answers to. If any word leaked out as a result of his needless disclosure, anything that resulted in harm to either Pop Holland or Dondero, he swore he'd come back to the *Express* and feed a few people here through one of their noisy presses, starting with the publisher! Although, to be honest, if anything unfortunate did occur, the fault would be his alone, as was the fix Dondero was in.

There was an abrupt rap on the door and it was opened without the visitor waiting for permission. The man who entered did so in stumping manner, as if his legs had been bound at the knees. He was an elderly man, stocky, with work clothes that had seen countless washings, and an ink-stained apron across his waist that he wore like a guerdon for services rendered in many a publishing battle. A neatly folded cap of newsprint hid his graying hair, a tribute to the origami talents of American pressmen; his huge gray

171

mustache hid all but red-veined cheeks. Tiny blue eyes peered out cautiously from beneath bushy eyebrows of indeterminate color. A huge curved pipe, unlit, hung from the corner of his mouth, touching his chin. He nodded to Maxwell as if the two of them were alone in the room.

"Y'wanted to see me, Mr. Maxwill?"

"Yes, Mac." Maxwell made no attempt to introduce Reardon, but pointed to the pasted-up note on his desk. "What do you think of this?"

Maxwell leaned over the thing, making no attempt to straighten it out. "It's a piss-poor paste-up job," he said, mostly under his breath. "Me grandson would have done better."

"Forget the paste-up job," Maxwell said impatiently. "I want your opinion on the printing, and the type. And the paper. Can you—I mean, do you have any idea of those?"

McDougal looked around shrewdly at the stranger, and then back to Maxwell. "Can I touch the thing?"

"You can touch it," Reardon said. McDougal's eyes remained fixed on Maxwell. "You can touch it, Mac," the publisher said, and smiled at Reardon. Reardon shrugged. He had a feeling he should have let Roy Gentry handle the entire investigation of the note. Time was passing and they were getting nowhere.

McDougal picked it up, studied the printing closely, his one hand pinching the paper the letters were pasted on. He looked up. "What d'you want to know?"

"Everything," Reardon said without much hope of a useful answer. "Can you identify the type? Or the paper?"

"Oh, aye," McDougal said. Reardon sat more erect. Maybe his visit wasn't going to be such a waste as he had feared. "It's from a shopping broadsheet; anyone can see that."

"Shopping broadsheet?" Reardon had come to his feet and was standing beside the stocky printer. McDougal cocked an eye at the interloper and then shrugged. If Maxwell didn't mind the stranger butting in constantly, why should he?

"That's right," he said, and took his pipe from his mouth to point with the stem. "Those numbers are probably the price of cheese, or eggs, or something. The job was set up with phototype, probably on aluminum plates, judging from the tone of definition.

172

Printed on a web press, probably. And the paper." He rustled it again between his fingers. "Twenty-eight pound circular stock, cheapest stuff around. Even cheaper than the newsprint we use, which is thirty-pound."

Reardon felt a sudden stir of excitement.

"Assuming it was printed in the San Francisco area," he said, "how many shops would you say are equipped with presses capable of doing work of that nature?"

"Plenty. Too many." McDougal shrugged and shoved his pipe back somewhere beneath his mustache. "Including those around the other side of the bay, I'd guess at fifteen. Maybe more."

"And just in the city proper?"

"Oh, maybe eight."

"And is there a list of them anywhere? Who would know who they are?"

Maxwell broke in. "They're in the phone book, I imagine, but McDougal would probably know as well as anyone. He's worked about every shop in the area, haven't you, Mac?"

McDougal nodded; he seemed to be pleased to be labeled a rolling stone.

"Oh, aye. I've worked plenty of them, but I know them all. I've been president of the union three times, and treasurer twice. I've seen them come up and seen them go broke." He looked at Maxwell calmly. "Newspapers, too . . ."

Reardon mentally crossed his fingers and asked his final question.

"Mr. McDougal, do you know of any shop, the kind of shop that might have produced that"—he pointed to the note still in McDougal's hand—"where there is someone working, in a supervisory position, I imagine, or more likely the owner himself, who has a beard, and smokes cigars, and has a small accomp—I mean, a small person—working with him closely, a person who is maybe five-foot-four?"

McDougal frowned at him. Up until the moment he had tolerated the stranger and his questions, but it seemed to him that now the man was getting damnably nosey. "And who might you be?"

"It's all right," Maxwell said. "He's the police." He was sitting up eagerly, his deep blue eyes sparkling with excitement. "Well? Would you know?"

"Oh, aye," McDougal said, and laid the note down on the desk again. "That'd be George Morrison, who owns the Neighborhood Print Works, over on Galvez. Mob money in the place, if you ask me. Bunch of goons working there. It's a scab shop We've had our troubles with Morrison, the sweet-talking thug!" He looked around for a place to spit, found none, and swallowed. "The little guy's probably Harry Wittwer. He drives for Morrison. Big George doesn't like to drive."

Reardon looked at the stocky printer unbelievingly. It had been that easy!

CHAPTER 15

Tuesday—12:00 NOON

Chief Boynton marched through the closely set desks as if they were obstacles to be overcome, following a prim Miss Tenefly, with Captain Tower on their heels. Miss Tenefly tapped once on the door of the corner office and then opened it, permitting her guests to enter. Once they had been properly delivered, she closed the door and returned to her desk, prepared—as anyone working for Mr. Maxwell had to be prepared—for anything.

Inside the office, Chief Boynton acknowledged the introductions and then frowned at the lieutenant.

"All right," he said quietly. "What's this all about? And if you've got something to report, why not at the Hall?"

"Because I think we can save ourselves a lot of trouble, with Mr. Maxwell's help," Reardon said. He was standing with his back to the window, looking at the chief evenly. He had had plenty of time since his call to the Hall to work things out. "If you'll just take a seat . . ."

Chief Boynton looked for a moment as if he might object, but then he shrugged and sat down. Captain Tower considered his subordinate a moment and then found a chair and followed suit. Lieutenant Reardon had always done a good job, and the captain had a feeling this case was no exception. Reardon could almost read his mind. Well, he thought, it's a damn good thing the captain doesn't know how much luck played in this one!

"All right," he said. "With the help of the *Express*, we've located the people we believe kidnapped Pop Holland. There's very little room for doubt. The man in charge is named George Morrison, and the small man who ran down the wino in Pop's car is named Harry Wittwer. Morrison runs a small printing plant called the Neighborhood Print Works, over on Galvez. Wittwer is his driver; Morrison apparently doesn't like to drive. We think Pop and Dondero might be held there, at the—"

"Dondero!" It came as a chorus from both Tower and Boynton.

"Yes, sir. Dondero took Lazaretti out of the cell block, it's true, but he didn't torture or kill him. Morrison and Wittwer did that. Don took the man out to trade him for Pop Holland, and—well, the kidnapper has him, too." And the statement, Reardon told himself, was true; it didn't seem the time to go into details that had been abridged. "As I started to say, Pop Holland and Don may be in the building on Galvez, or they may not. My guess is they are. Now, we could surround the building with a dozen squad cars and end up with a shoot-'em-up, and somebody would get hurt, and that includes Pop and Dondero. Or, we can play it smart and ask Mr. Maxwell for his help."

Boynton was quiet, trying to absorb the information he had just received. Tower frowned. "Mr. Maxwell's help? How?"

"Well," Reardon said, "I spoke with Davidson while you were on your way over here, and he'll have men on the Neighborhood Print Works in the next fifteen minutes. They're probably there now. They'll be instructed not to be obvious. There are men on foot and cars, both, but if Dave knows his job—and he does—nobody at the print works will have any idea they're covered. Then, as soon as Morrison and Wittwer leave—"

"How do you know they're there?"

Reardon smiled. "Because Miss Tenefly, Mr. Maxwell's invaluable secretary, just had a wrong number and spoke with Morrison. She was looking for the Neighborhood Dry Cleaning Company to register a complaint, and she wouldn't believe they weren't giving her a run around until she spoke with the boss. No, Morrison's there."

176

"And what makes you think they'll leave?"

"That's Mr. Maxwell's part of the job." Reardon looked at Maxwell. "Ready?"

"Ready," the little man said. His eyes were twinkling with delight. He picked up the telephone, asked for an outside line, and dialed. There was a short wait; then the telephone at the other end was raised.

"Neighborhood Print Works."

The humor died from Maxwell's face. He looked to be exactly what he was; a tough experienced publisher. Tower and Boynton watched the small man with curiosity; Reardon smiled. Maxwell's voice was harsh.

"I want to speak with Mr. Morrison."

"Who wants to talk to him?"

"This is Ira Maxwell, publisher of the *Express*. Please tell Mr. Morrison this call is extremely important." He cupped the receiver and winked jovially at the others, then straightened his face and removed his hand as another voice came on the line. "Morrison? Is this George Morrison? How are you? We've never met, but I've heard a lot about you, and I think you can help me out. And, in return, I think I can help you out."

"Help you out? How?" Morrison sounded slightly amused by the call.

"I understand you run a nonunion shop. Well, we're sitting here, me and my lawyers, talking about just that. We're about to come up for negotiations and these damn fools here are ready to give away the whole damn plant! I thought if you could come over and join us for an hour or so, maybe you could give us some idea of how you operate. Damned if I'm going to give everything I've worked for to some damned union . . . !"

"I don't know . . ." There was a brief pause while everyone in the room waited tensely. Then Morrison spoke. "And just what would be the quid pro quo you mentioned if I did help you out?"

Maxwell was quite prepared. He had a pencil in one hand and doodled as he spoke.

"You buy your newsprint through Western American, don't you? Of course you do. I happen to be a major stockholder in Western American. How do you think I've stayed in business

177

as long as I have against such competition as the *Chronicle* and the *Examiner* if I didn't have an edge? Now, we had a board meeting of Western American not very long ago, and the question came up of a price rise—"

Morrison laughed, genuinely amused. "I'm not afraid of any price rise."

"I don't believe you understand," Maxwell said, and Reardon was amazed at the toughness that had crept into the little man's voice, a toughness he was sure Morrison would recognize. "The reason we are thinking of a price rise is that we have overcut our forests, and the concensus was we should raise prices and reduce output for a few years. The oil producers have done very well with this method, and we believe it would have equal advantages for us. That, of course, would mean dropping some customers . . ." He allowed his voice to drift off.

There was silence at the other end of the line for several moments. Then Morrison said quietly, "I'll be in your office in twenty minutes, Mr. Maxwell."

"Thank you," Maxwell said graciously, but he was talking to a dead line. He hung up and turned to the others, smiling faintly. "Morrison will be here in twenty minutes."

Reardon looked at that bright, shrewd, smiling face with the sharp blue eyes and hoped he would never have to face the little man on a business deal. He reached behind him to his belt holster and removed his service revolver. He checked it carefully, slid it into his outside jacket pocket for easy access, then seated himself, waiting. Captain Tower did the same with his revolver and also placed it in his side pocket. Chief Boynton merely came to his feet and moved to the window, staring out.

The minutes ticked by. Then there was a rap on the door; it opened and a large bearded man stood on the threshold. His glance passed the other three men in the room and fastened on Maxwell. "You're Mr. Maxwell . . . ?" he started to say, and then did a rapid double take, turning swiftly to face Reardon. "You're . . . !" His hand went to his pocket, but before either of the others could draw their guns, Chief Boynton had moved swiftly.

178

His big hand slapped Morrison across the face with all his might. Morrison stood there a moment, dazed, and then slid to the floor, unconscious.

"Too many guns around, these days," Boynton said briefly, and bent down to frisk the man on the floor.

Tuesday—12:30 P.M.

Harry Wittwer sat behind the wheel of the large Cadillac and bit his lip. Whatever labor problem this Maxwell had, Harry sincerely hoped George could solve, because the one thing they had to have was newsprint, and getting it on a moment's notice from some other company than Western American was damn near impossible. And without the "Neighborhood Shopping News," they would have plenty of problems—

He suddenly looked up, aware that someone was speaking to him. It was a man dressed in work clothes, crossing the street in front of the car, pointing downward.

"Hey, mister," Jennings said. "You're getting a flat."

Harry started to open the door, his back turned to the sidewalk, and then froze as a gun dug into his ribs.

"Just sit real nice and quiet and don't reach for anything," Johnny Merchant said pleasantly, "or I'll take your pillow away and you won't be able to see over the steering wheel."

Tuesday—6:00 P.M.

The party that was going on this time was taking place in the front room of Marty's Oyster House, in a booth in the rear, and since Jan was present the service was not only prompt but waiters seemed to be standing in line to handle her every whim. The fact that this meant they also had to handle the irresponsible whims of the two men with her was unfortunate, but with one accord the waiters felt it was worth it. Dolls like that didn't walk into

179

Marty's every day of the week! Reardon had been telephoning from the cashier's extension; he came back and sat down next to Jan, taking one of her hands in his.

"Pop'll be fine," he said, pleased. "The hospital doesn't expect any complications from the finger, and outside of that he's just tired. They think he'll be out and around in a few days."

"Great!" Dondero said. He was wearing dark glasses to hide a badly battered eye, and his split lip made drinking painful, although that did not prevent him from drinking. He just drank carefully. He set his glass down and patted his lip gently. "When I walked in on him and he pulled the exact same line you'd said he'd pull, I was so surprised I said, 'Shut up, Pop, for Christ's sake!' instead of using my head."

Reardon looked at him critically. "It looks to me like you did use your head. Or somebody did."

"Somebody sure did," Dondero said bitterly, and reached up gingerly to touch the edge of his eye. He thought of something. "Hey! Who got to talk to Patrone?"

"Several of us," Reardon said grimly. "In depth. The two and a half kilos were in a suitcase at the checkroom of the Mark Hopkins. At least they picked a stash point that was classy." He frowned. "The thing that surprises me the most about the whole thing is why Morrison bought Maxwell's story so easily. Why should he get so up-tight about not being able to buy some paper?"

"I can tell you all about that," Dondero said. "You don't think I wasted all my time just being a punching bag, do you? I listened, pal; and they didn't worry too much about talking in front of me, either, because they also mentioned what they were going to do with me and Pop once they got their hands on Patrone. It didn't involve survival."

"So what's the secret?"

"So they had a good setup," Dondero said half-admiringly. "The shopping news gimmick was legitimate, and for all I know it may have even made them a buck or two, but it was also the basis of their distribution setup. They delivered the papers by hand, and while that meant they couldn't stuff mailboxes—because

180

that's against the postal laws, you know—they didn't want to stuff mailboxes, anyway. They wanted to drop them behind screens, or shove them under doors, or even hand them over to people who opened the door when their delivery boy came up on the stoop. And inside those papers that were accepted by hand, or shoved under a door completely, they had a small glassine envelope pasted, with a deal of horse in it." He grinned. "I'd give eight to five some narc, doing a surveillance, probably saw the stuff handed over under his nose and thought nothing of it."

"Cute," Reardon said. "Well, it's all busted up, now, and maybe we can all get some sleep." He pressed Jan's hand. "Want to eat here, honey?"

"Why not?" Jan said, happy to be with him and pleased to see him relaxing. "The service is wonderful."

Dondero choked on his drink.

"Why not, indeed?" Reardon asked, smiling. He picked up a menu from the stack behind the napkin holder and then handed it to Jan. "You order for me, honey. I've got one more call to make."

"Hurry back."

"I'll be there before the waiter," Reardon said, and walked back to the telephone.

Tuesday—6:20 P.M.

Sawicki, proprietor and principal hustler of his pool emporium, wondered what he could possibly have done to irritate Lady Luck to make her treat him like this! A miscue on an absolutely-dead-as-Kelsey-combination-break ball had to rank with the *Titanic* as a major disaster! Now look at the goddamn table! It looked like a couple of high school kids were playing rotation, for crissakes! Sawicki tried to control his temper, retreating bearlike to one of the high stools against the wall, shaking his head.

Porky Frank smiled gently and studied the layout, chalking his cue carefully as he did so. Sawicki did not offer his largess so frequently that one could afford to be careless in the acceptance thereof. His eye went from ball to ball, planning strategy and position, and when his plan was completed, he bent down to the table, prepared to put Sawicki out of his misery as quickly as possible. At that moment the telephone rang.

Sawicki leaned his cue against the wall and went to answer it. His tiny molelike eyes lit up at the sound of the familiar voice; he forced himself to present a poker face as he turned to address his opponent.

"Telephone, Porky," he said in his gravel voice. "For you."

"Oh? Thanks." Porky Frank laid his cue on a nearby abandoned table, being more protective of his property than Sawicki, and walked over to the phone, raising the receiver. Sawicki politely refrained from listening. Porky smiled at him and spoke. "Hello?"

"Porky?"

"Ah, Mr. R! What can I do for you?"

"I tried your apartment, but I guess you'd already left."

"A reasonable assumption," Porky said in a congratulatory tone. "Is anything new on the you-know-what?"

"Quite a bit," Reardon said. "I would have let you read all about it in the *Express*, except I remember you don't read newspapers. Well, you'll be pleased to know that Mike Holland is in the hospital—under our care—and that a couple of bad boys named George Morrison and Harry Wittwer are being held for kidnapping, among other things."

"Congratulations," Porky said, honestly pleased. "Morrison and Wittwer, eh?"

"You know them?"

"Only by reputation," Porky said. He thought a moment and nodded. "That would explain a few things. . . ."

"Such as?"

"Well, you recall at our last meeting I mentioned a temporary lack of powdered Nirvana in the marketplace? As I hear it, George Morrison was one of the lads involved in that field."

"We know," Reardon said, pleased for once to be ahead of Porky. "Little Harry told us all about it. The mob arranged the incoming package, via Patrone. Morrison knew about it, naturally, and decided—when he heard the courier was in jail—on a nice lit-

182

tle hijack scheme, all on his own. My guess is that both Morrison and Wittwer will pray for a long, long sentence. There'll be people waiting for them when they get out."

"If they wait," Porky said. "I hear they're a restless bunch, at times. I imagine that Morrison heard the courier was in jail by reading the papers?"

"That's right. There was a squib about it. And if it makes you any happier, that column 'View from Nob Hill' did mention that I was in charge of the dinner. And Morrison knew me from the few times he'd seen my picture in the papers. I gather he preferred to deal with a known element."

"Like a policeman who puts things off to the last minute," Porky said. "Well, I'm glad you finally got around to looking up that columnist. You see? Listen to the old pro and you'll never go wrong. That, Mr. R, will cost you."

"And that, Mr. P, is worth it," Reardon said, smiling. Why tell Porky the way Mr. Maxwell and his organization helped was not exactly the way Porky imagined? "Now, go back to your game, and good luck."

"Thank you," Porky said, and hung up. He stood staring at the telephone for a moment and then walked slowly back to the pool table. Sawicki looked up in all innocence.

"You got to go away, Porky?" he asked, barely able to hide the welling hope in his gravelly voice.

Porky smiled at him in gentle fashion and retrieved his cue from the adjoining table.

"Not tonight, Josephine," he said, and bent over the rail to make his first shot.